Tales from *Luna*, The Lone Wolf

BLOOD OF AN ALPHA

Forest Wells

Blood of an Alpha

Edited by: "Edge of the World Editing"
https://www.fiverr.com/share/A0jKVq
edgeoftheworldediting@gmail.com

Cover image by: "Makangeni"
https://www.deviantart.com/makangeni

Cover and Interior design by: Éric Desmarais
https://www.EricDesmarais.ca

First Edition
ISBN E-book: 978-1-7337124-2-2
ISBN Paperback: 978-1-7337124-3-9

To the current and former girls of Girl Scout Troops 414 and 103-

There! You got another story with the wolves! Leave me alone! :D

To my mother and Jane Lindskold-

Your loyalty and support keep me writing.

And to the victims of 9/11-

Without whom this book, and this author, would not exist.

Contents

Introduction

I always tell authors, "All that matters is that the story be told, in full, the way it needs to be told." When I began my revisions for "Luna, The Lone Wolf," I realized that in a way, I could only pick one of those.

The way it needed to be told meant it could not be told in full. I couldn't spend the time to show the forming of Toltan's pack, nor the early months of Luna's life. Things moved too slowly with no real benefit. To say nothing of showing Estrella's tale being far too much of a separation to include.

And yet, those stories needed to be told.

I had never deleted my discarded pages (a practice I HIGHLY suggest all authors adopt). There was still a valid story to be had, more so when I put the focus on Martol and Toltan, and then later on Estrella and Carlin respectively. So, while "Luna" was being refined, I also adapted the rejected pages into their own stories. It wasn't in the original plan, but in writing circles I am what's called a "pantser". I write by the seat of my pants, no plan to be had. I just write, I let the story tell itself, and on occasion I get to nudge it down a certain path.

But most important of all; I finally got to finish the FULL story. Not just Luna, not just Toltan, not just Estrella, but the combined tale of these wolves.

The other half of that duality is the annoying fact that these wolves are not accurate to real wolves. There have been some serious three-way brawls between me, the story, and the muse over that, but the story eventually won. While there is a lot of accurate research that has been infused into the stories, to tell the tale the way it needed to be told, we couldn't be fully accurate to real wolves.

A prime example; the idea of "alpha" does not exist in a pack. It's not "yes Mighty Alpha, I will follow you." It's more like, "yes Dad." What we've seen as "alpha" is more like the father or mother of the pack. Like any large family, the eldest parent leads. It's not a hierarchy. It's just a family living together. Though I admit I am uncertain what happens to a pack when their breeding pair dies. As far as I could determine, sometimes a loner will come in and mate with a member and take the lead, or the pack will completely dissolve. But even this I suspect is not the full list of things that can happen when the parents of a pack die. For one thing, I believe there are some packs who have held the same territory much longer than the maximum life span of any wild wolf.

Regardless of the truth, I hope my readers can forgive me for writing not fully accurate wolves. It's not an easy thing to admit that I knowingly wasn't accurate about something like that. But the story couldn't be told the way it needed to be told if I strove for that kind of accuracy. Luna's entire journey wouldn't touch people the way it has, nor would the journeys contained within this book weigh as heavy, if I had. I guess all I can do is hope the journeys were worth the inconsistencies.

In the mean time, there is one last question I'm sure many of you are asking; is this it? Is this the last we'll see of these wolves? My answer is; I don't know either. As far as I can see, it looks like it is, but I remind you that I have no control over my stories. We may yet see them again, or we may never see them again. I don't know any more than you do.

But I can say that this isn't the last pack animal you'll see me do. Nor the last wolf. I have many more tales to tell and journeys to share. But for now, I think it's time we let these wolves live their lives in peace.

After all, Luna especially has earned it.

In the mean time, I'd like to offer a big thank you to my beta readers, who helped me make this collection the best it could possibly be.

Laurel

Michelle

Kieran

Blood of an Alpha

Prologue

Wolfor: Creator of all wolves, the alpha wolf, from which the name is taken.

Believed to be a grand wolf himself, though no one knows what he looks like. It's said that when he created wolves, he left them to run the wilds of the Earth until the day comes they can run no more. When death comes, wolves journey to Wolfor's sacred dwelling on the moon. Known as "Luna", it is the only land to bear a name. There, wolves will spend the rest of time in Wolfor's territory, where he will guard, protect, and provide for them.

While on Earth, wolves are still watched over by Wolfor, at times acting in their favor. He will bear his fangs when they are threatened, he will share his kills when they are weak or starving, and he will lend his fur when they are scared or alone. He is ever watchful, ever protecting, and always there for those he created. Never has he forgotten them, yet the trials they face will better prepare them for their eternity spent with him.

It is unclear what it takes to earn his favor, though many suspect he does choose who will or will not be alpha. Then again, just because a wolf is his choice does not guarantee that he or she will be the one to lead. In such cases, the pack almost always suffers. For those not chosen are missing the one thing a leader needs. That unidentifiable element. The fire, the drive, the devotion, the courage.

The blood of an alpha.

***

"Toltan! Toltan, get back here!"

Toltan didn't listen. He didn't care. He wanted to see the world. The smells coming from outside the den were too enticing not to explore. The challenge to evade his parents made it all the more irresistible. He'd already snuck past the den guards. Most of the rest of the pack were out hunting, leaving only those wolves lounging in the gathering area to deal with.

He kept to the shadows, using his dark grey pelt to blend in with them. He saw a clear path through the shrubs. No wolves there. A few more steps and—

"Gotcha!"

Toltan felt jaws plant him to the ground. He cried out in pain... that he soon realized wasn't there. His ears still went flat and his tail melded with his rear end as he looked back to see who had caught him. He saw a young female not yet full grown. She had thick silver fur that was smooth as ice, but her eyes entranced him even more. They were hard right now, for she was glaring at him, but he saw a softness there too. *How did I miss a wolf that pretty?*

"Martol?" his mother called. She was breathing hard as she appeared next to the female. When she saw what Martol had caught, she sighed relief. "Thank you. I was afraid he'd gotten clean away."

"He almost did," Martol said with an amused ruff. She returned to glaring at Toltan. "What does this make, five times now?"

"S... S... seven." Toltan said, trying his best to look innocent.

Martol flicked an ear before looking back at Toltan's mother. "Jilsina, I do not envy you and Mouler."

"I said the same thing to your father when he was alpha," Jilsina said. "I'm beginning to wonder if Wolfor took it as a challenge."

"I wouldn't mind having pups some day. Though you'll forgive me if I hope I never have a pup like him."

"Careful what you wish for. You may end up with much worse." Jilsina stood over her pup while Martol held her own vigil. "You however, need to learn some wisdom. That forest is dangerous for one so young."

Toltan found his courage, or more foolishness. "I'm not afraid! I want to see what's out there. I want to hunt the things I smell."

"You will when you're big enough to catch them. At your size, you bite a rabbit, he's likely to drag you with him."

"Rabbits don't eat wolves."

"But eagles do," Martol said. Jilsina glanced back at her, causing Martol to lower her ears until Jilsina turned hers forward in approval.

"She has a point," Jilsina said. "There are many things you do not yet know."

"I want to learn!" Toltan said. "I want to—"

"Enough!" Jilsina's growl forced even Martol's ears to fall. "Someday, you will be strong. You may even take your father's place as alpha, but until that day, you must wait and learn. As for today, you will remain within the den. You will not leave without an adult, for any reason, at any time. Am I understood?"

Jilsina glared at him, still as a stone, hot as an inferno. The death stance the pack called it. As in you only challenge it if you want to die.

Toltan shrank in size, but did tick his ears forward. "Yes mother."

"Use my name," she ruffed. "It's time you pups started to apply the rules you learn."

"Yes... Jilsina."

Jilsina ruffed in his face before looking back at Martol again. Martol's ears shifted uneasily, to which Jilsina ruffed amusement.

"Take him back to the den please. Make sure he stays there."

Chapter 1

Toltan buried his nose in the carpet of flowers, inhaling their scent while fighting back sneezes that might damage the source. Such delicate, soft, sweet scents, others somehow musty, still more almost sour, yet no less appealing. Such an array of smells, no wonder he couldn't make sense of them on the wind as a pup. They'd become a jumbled mess by the time his nose ever touched them. That is until now, when he was better able to enjoy them.

"You find that scent yet?"

Solas. His almost twin brother, at least by fur color, but that's as far as the relationship went. Even then, Solas' coat had more dark grey than his, and Solas' cream underside and legs bordered on brown. Toltan meanwhile had developed a white and cream underside, which extended up to his forehead and muzzle.

Personality wise, they couldn't be more different. Toltan didn't mind taking a moment to enjoy life. Solas meanwhile...

"Toltan! We need to find that deer before it gets back to its herd."

Toltan had to wonder if Solas would actually drop when he died, or if he'd keep right on hunting.

"No luck yet," Toltan said.

He heard an annoyed growl from Solas followed by a lot of snorting, only half of which was looking for the trail. The other half was for Toltan. The rest of the hunting party had more or less ignored them both in favor of the hunt.

Toltan's ears did turn back when he heard someone else approach. He gave a soft growl of his own when Martol pushed past him to check where he'd been sniffing. She ignored him of course, as she often had since he'd crossed from pup to adult.

"You find something else?" she asked. "All I can find is flowers."

Toltan ruffed amusement. At least she was talking to him for a change. "Me too. Sweet aren't they?"

"So you have a thing for flowers huh?"

"Sure. What's wrong with that?"

Martol sneezed after a deep sniff, and Toltan wasn't sure she didn't do it on purpose. "You're a wolf. We track prey so we can eat it. These have no bearing on us."

"Just because I'm a deadly hunter doesn't mean I can't appreciate a little beauty. After all, you're pretty good looking yourself."

That got her. Martol tried to glare at him, but her softer ears gave away her blush. She tried to force them forward in aggression. A softer flick of amusement came out instead.

"Come on," she said. "We still have a kill to find. Unless of course, you intend to eat those things."

Toltan ruffed a chuckle. *Nice dodge.* Though he had to admit, he really should continue the hunt.

He left the flowers behind in favor of where the original trail had turned through them. He and Martol hit on the same thought at once as both went straight through the field until the flowers ended. They didn't need long afterward to find where the deer had continued. Fresh blood is always easy for a wolf to find.

"Solas, this way," Toltan called.

He led the way through thickening trees as the trail darted between them. Despite the bite they'd landed, this one buck had covered a lot of ground. Toltan found himself trotting along the trail, dripping drool as he imagined the bounty he'd find. He wouldn't get much considering the large size of the pack, but that didn't keep him from thinking about it.

The blood drops grew in size and frequency as they moved. Surely it couldn't keep this pace for long. It had to be getting weak. Then again, it didn't need long. The herd wasn't far. All it needed to do was last long enough to catch up with them.

A crash snapped Toltan's ears and head up. Another hoof clap sent him and the others running toward it. The claps grew louder, and his pace faster. It was staggering! Only thing that could explain it making so much noise. The chase and the wound had finally caught up with it. Toltan tore through brush to make sure it didn't crawl back to its herd.

His enthusiasm almost sent him charging into its antlers. He had to dig his claws deep to stop, then dig again to avoid getting mauled by a swipe from the buck's head. It caught only his tail, and it slithered through unharmed.

Toltan might have been caught off guard, but he had never stopped thinking. After escaping harm, he planted his paws and turned around as the hunting party drew the buck's attention. All nine snapped low, feinting mostly to get it to expose its neck, but its attention had exposed something else. Toltan charged in as it stomped a tail's width short of Solas. Before it remembered him, Toltan had gotten in behind and sent his muzzle stabbing at the buck's hind quarters.

His fangs landed where he'd aimed them; right onto the creature's genitals. Toltan planted and pulled as hard as he could, tearing out a hunk of flesh from the buck's hind-quarters. His face was drenched in a glop of blood as he pulled away before it could kick him. It turned to face him, but he and the party had retreated well outside any possible attack range. They knew what a strike of that kind did. As the ground was stained by the buck's blood, it staggered, tried to keep it's footing, then collapsed as the blood loss claimed its energy, and soon after its life.

"Toltan," Solas said between pants, "you can be flighty sometimes, but your fangs could catch a hummingbird's tongue."

"You're welcome," Toltan said.

Solas stepped forward to lead the feasting, as well as choosing parts to bring back to the pack.

His fangs never touched the kill.

Solas yipped pain as another wolf tackled him before anyone saw him arrive. The shock prevented the rest of the party from seeing the other wolves until most found themselves in a fight for their lives. Thankfully the attackers weren't able to use their advantage. The hunting party shed the initial attack and forced an even ten-on-ten brawl. Snaps were traded all at once, others fought paws on the shoulders, trying to get an angle.

Toltan found himself doing the latter with a female bigger than he was. They stood almost upright as they both tried to land a bite on the other. Toltan was able to strike fast and accurate, but even his best efforts could only block a bite or land a meaningless blow on legs or fur.

Then at one point, the female pushed too hard for him to counter. Toltan was forced to drop to avoid landing on his back, which allowed her to lock her jaws onto the back of his neck instead. Mostly scruff, thank Wolfor, but it still hurt, and it still had him in big trouble. She tried to push him down, and he pushed back knowing that if she got him down, she'd end him.

He tugged hard trying to get away, but she stayed with him every time. He kept pulling anyway because he knew that if he didn't, sooner or later, she would readjust and kill him. He tried to plant and pull again, except this time his right legs caught the dead legs of the deer. They slipped off, sending him sliding onto his side.

He expected the female to go for his underbelly, but at the same time he'd fallen, she'd pulled up just a second to reposition. When she came down to try another push, her body expected to find Toltan still fighting her. Instead it found no resistance at all. The mis-proportion of force sent her muzzle into the ground with all the force meant for Toltan, with her head catching some of the blow as well. She yipped more in surprise than pain, but the pain was enough to loosen her jaws and send her head spinning.

Toltan had only a second of surprise to get over. The moment he recognized his advantage, he used his fangs with lethal accuracy. His first strike punctured an eye. His second snapped a foreleg in half. His third landed on the throat, and stayed there until the female fell limp on the ground.

Toltan snapped his head up to check the status of the battle. Much of his own pack had faired as well or better than he did. Solas, despite gashes on his shoulder, was taking down his opponent, while Martol danced around hers like a hummingbird darting between flowers. She struck with equal quickness. Though not as well as Toltan did, she still left her mark.

He decided to end the dance to free her for the others. He charged in, found the tail of the enemy up, and let his hunter blood do the rest. Once again, he took aim, and his fangs followed. Just like the deer, he went for the genital area, found his mark, and tore a gash that drew a strong stream of blood. The enemy wolf didn't get to bleed out however, as Martol ended him herself while he cried out in pain.

They both went looking for the next opponent, yet found the remaining attackers retreating into the distance. Solas led the chase until they'd gone well beyond their pack's borders. Satisfied they'd run them off, the hunting party returned to claim their kill and care for their wounds. Many were bleeding, all were panting hard, and two of their own lay dead from the attack. The rival party in contrast had lost half a dozen, not counting those whose wounds might claim them later. *Still too many,* Toltan thought.

"What was that about?" Toltan said aloud. "I've never seen such aggression from another pack."

"I may have part of the answer," Martol said. She was just beside the kill, sniffing at the bush the first wolf had jumped from. "They marked this bush recently. I think they thought they'd claimed this territory, and *we* were the intruders."

Solas examined the scent while Toltan checked the more serious of the wounded. Thank Wolfor again, they didn't appear to be life threatening. The worst were heavy bleeders that always looked worse than they were. Thorough cleaning would keep the wounds little more than scars.

Solas meanwhile snorted at the marked bush. "Mouler apparently needs to remark his borders."

"He did," Martol said. "Just yesterday."

"Then what would drive another pack to such aggression? Could it be the rage plague?"

"There's no way to know… unless… unless one of us—"

"Don't say it! Mouler has enough to deal with without the idea of one of his pack going mad. Perhaps they were simply foolish enough to think they could claim the territory."

Toltan prayed he was right, but something within said he wasn't. He couldn't find a source beyond a nagging feeling that wouldn't go away. As much as it worried him, without the source, he could do little about it now.

For the moment at least, he gladly pushed the thought away as the party lifted their heads briefly in a long howl of mourning. They'd lost only two, but a loss is a loss. In a way, Toltan cursed himself that he'd almost forgotten about them. Martol hadn't, as she had been the first to begin the howl. The group joined on her tail, grieving the loss of their fellow wolves.

Sadly, the wild life does not allow grief to dominate. The pack still needed to be cared for. After marking the borders again themselves, the party finally got around to eating their kill. The group ate with more energy than normal, a touch energized by the blood spent to win the kill. The bloodlust got to Martol though, as she had to be reminded by Solas' fangs that the kidneys weren't hers to take. Toltan satisfied himself with a thigh, and let each mouthful slide down with smooth joy.

As the party started gathering the left-overs for the pack, he had to push the female he'd killed off to get at it. It was only then he noticed her state. She was so thin that her ribs were showing, and where her fur wasn't matted, it was thin or weak as if half the strands that should be there were missing. Her jaws were also pale, and not from recent death either. A glance at the other bodies as the party passed them showed the same signs of malnourishment. Now he knew why his instincts rejected Solas' reasons. The attackers weren't disputing territory, they were desperate for a meal.

Yet that didn't make sense either. Toltan knew this forest. There was more than enough game for them beyond Mouler's border. How could a pack of any size get that thin?

A crack of thunder drew everyone's ears in the direction the other wolves had fled. It was so distant at first Toltan wasn't sure he'd heard it. The fact that there wasn't a cloud in the sky didn't help much. Worse yet were the birds that came soon after. Flocks of several breeds, squawking as they flew, very much on edge. Whatever the thunder was, it wasn't something they were used to.

Martol ruffed through her mouthful of meat. When the party looked to her, she moved on toward their meeting area. Most followed without question, while Solas and Toltan traded looks that said "since when did she make alpha?" They also decided to let it be via the same method. She had the right idea. They had what they came for, and hanging around now would only put them at risk. Assuming of course there was risk to hang around for.

Toltan felt sure there was, but he buried it under a lie to the contrary, at least for now.

Chapter 2

Mouler sniffed at the meat his hunting party had brought back. After the tale they'd told him, he wasn't all that confident. His pelt of soft grey bordered by brown kept trying to decide if it should rise or not. Oh not for the kill. For something much more unsettling.

"You're sure they didn't have the rage plague?" he said, staring over the meat at Toltan.

Toltan ticked his ears forward in the affirmative. "None of the other signs were there. They were aggressive, but far from disoriented."

"Now that you say that, I agree," Martol said. "I saw that loner try to fight off the mountain lion. These wolves were far more coordinated than that."

"'That loner'," Mouler said gravely, "was your father, and he was in the late stages of the illness. The early signs are not always so apparent."

Martol cringed, but only for a moment. She'd never really gotten to know the wolf that sired her. By the time she did, he'd been driven away to protect the pack. The combination had created an unnatural detachment Mouler wished he could cure. Then again, considering what happened to him, perhaps it was best she didn't have the emotional scars.

"Forgive me, Mouler," Martol said, barely flinching, "but even if they were infected, they never touched the kill."

"You did," Mouler said, "after you killed them."

"Oh for goodness sake, eat it or don't. Either way, I have wounds to lick."

Martol left without so much as a lowered ear in response. Mouler started to growl at her, but his mate, Jilsina, a wolf of black fur with tiny bits of white on her belly, hips, and sides of her neck, stopped him.

"She's right, Mouler. Either eat the kill or don't, but don't waste the day deciding whether it's safe or not."

Mouler shifted his growl to her, which as usual Jilsina ignored. She took her share into the den beside a massive oak tree, no doubt to give the pups their first exposure to it, followed by their first taste of the regurgitated version. That left the old alpha alone with his meal and his son.

The latter had already flopped onto his belly not a body length away to care for his own wounds. The rest of the hunting party had also dispersed to rest from the day's hunt. Mouler envied them. They didn't know what he knew. The rage plague was just a way to avoid thinking about it.

Thunder from a cloudless sky. Mouler's father had told him of such things. *Mere legends* he thought, much like the tales of Wolfor and his dwelling on the moon. Well, almost. Wolfor he believed in. The thunder... he never had until now.

Thunder on its own of course was little to worry about. Yet thunder combined with wolves in such a state, that was an entirely different situation. One he could not ignore no matter how much he wanted to.

Mouler's thoughts were interrupted when he saw jaws reaching for his meal. They belonged to Mesin, another of his sons from the same litter as Toltan, except this one's pelt was black as night, and he feared the mind beneath it might be just as dim. The only thing he really had going for him was he was huge by wolf standards, standing an ear's length taller than Mouler with a build to match. Yet, as is often the case in packs, size alone meant very little.

Mouler snapped his jaws onto Mesin's neck and thrust him into the ground with a snarl that shook them both. Mesin's tail tucked while he hugged the ground as if he might merge with it. Only when he added a soft whine did Mouler release him. Even then,

Mesin managed to make his bulk look smaller as he rolled onto his paws.

"Do not forget your place," Mouler said. "Find Solas. He'll have your share. And do not let me catch you sharing it with Lavila. As omega, her place is to eat last."

Now Mesin's ears shot up, though that's all that did. "She doesn't fit the position. She could be an alpha female."

"Lavila is too submissive. She bows before any pressure. That is why she serves the role so well. She is able to defuse tensions without over-stepping her place. If you spent more time among the pack truly observing, you'd see that."

"She could do that as alpha. She could even settle matters with the given authority."

"Then let her earn it. In the meantime, her place is of her own choosing, as is yours."

Mesin snorted, rose, and left. He stopped only to look back and say, "If I had 'my choice', I'd be alpha, and Lavila would be my mate. But you won't let me have either."

Mouler ignored the comment. Mesin made a noise bigger than he was, but he'd been mired in his place too long for it to mean anything. A shame really. Mesin wasn't that bad a hunter. The problem lay in his decision making. Mouler had seen him be quite foolish on hunts, at times to the point of almost getting killed while chasing a target as it regrouped with the herd. Despite his bulk, Mesin was remarkably agile, which is probably the only way he'd managed to survive his own foolishness. That and wolves watch out for each other. Even when a certain member is stupid.

While Mouler finally let himself eat the food his pack had brought him, he barely tasted it. It slid down his throat then vanished from memory. His mind was too busy worrying about the attackers. What could drive a pack to such desperation? Worse, just how desperate were they? Toltan described wolves in the worst of conditions. If they had pups that were somehow still alive, their alpha would be even more desperate. Being anywhere near a pack like that was dangerous. Sharing a border... he'd already lost two of his pack, and that was just the first encounter. If another one came, he might lose more.

That didn't count whatever threat, if any, this strange thunder posed.

As Mouler looked again at Toltan, he realized he had a chance to do something about one of the threats. He'd change how the pack moved and hunted, reducing the chances of any group being overpowered, but there was something else he could do too. Though Toltan had settled in to sleep, the twitching of his ears at Mouler's approach proved he was still awake. Mouler laid next to him without a word, offering a soft nuzzle on his muzzle as much to show affection as to get his attention.

Toltan shook the fog from his mind before turning his ears to his father. "Something wrong?"

Isn't that the question of the day? "Maybe. That's why I need you to listen. I need you to hear, understand, and remember. The life of the pack may well depend on it."

"Understand what? What are you talking about?"

"Something I'm still not sure is real. But if it is, what my father told me about it may help you defend us all from great harm."

***

Toltan was happy to have his alpha – no – his father, on the hunt with him. Mouler had been somewhat withdrawn since the last one, so it relieved Toltan to see him moving smooth and loose like he remembered. Okay, maybe Mouler wasn't being playful like he once was, but then, Toltan wasn't a pup anymore. No, Mouler was leading the hunt straight and firm, a mountain of a wolf, if only by aura. Everything one expected from an alpha.

Toltan followed close behind. He kept his nose to the air, but his ears remained on his alpha. Mouler checked each trail carefully, digging in the dirt some times, checking trees others, marking one as they passed. All without a word. The calm, quiet confidence of experience Toltan hadn't seen for some time.

It's just as well. The long conversation after the last hunt still had him unsettled. Legends of two-legged beasts, something about thunder, it was all so vague. He really didn't understand most of it, nor did he believe such beasts could exist. Were it not for Mouler's insistence, he might not have remembered any of it, much less stayed to listen. But he did, and he couldn't shake the feeling that he'd someday have to put it to use.

That day was not today however. Today he was on another hunt, this time with his father, and his brother. Mesin was, thank Wolfor, keeping his place behind Mouler and the better trackers for a change. Toltan didn't mind him really. He just didn't want him doing anything until it came time for the kill.

Then again, he didn't much care for the attention he was showing Lavila. It seemed to be extra intense for some reason, which only made it worse. With a pack as large as theirs and bearing a healthy alpha pair, no one should be courting anyone, least of all an omega. Were he alpha, Toltan would have done a lot more to stop it.

But he wasn't, so he let it be.

Instead, he returned full focus to his alpha. Mouler had stopped at the head of a game trail they used nearly every moon. Toltan expected him to tear off after a good target at any moment. Except Mouler continued to dig at the scent in front of him as if confused, or worried, about it's owner. When Mouler froze and looked down the path with erect ears, Toltan decided to risk a venture.

"What's wrong? Are there no scents?"

Mouler didn't move. "There are *too many* scents."

"Since when is an abundance of trails a problem?" Mesin asked. Toltan swallowed a growl. *Should have known it wouldn't last.*

"First; too many different trails. Second; too much fresh blood on it. Third; not all of it is prey. Some of it is wolf."

"And we have a dozen of our best with us. What is there to fear?"

Beyond the fact that we only have ten of our best, a decent omega, and one big risk? Toltan kept the thought to himself. Again, he wasn't alpha, as much as he wanted to be at the moment. He wanted to snap at Mesin to be sure he was listening, then explain as he would to a pup what there was to fear. He wanted to see if he could force sense into his brother's head. He did nothing, for it was not his place.

Mouler meanwhile largely ignored him. "There is always danger in a large change. Why so many herds in one place? Why so much blood? Where are the wolves I smell on the ground."

"You're being paranoid," Mesin said. "Wolfor will provide. We'll face the challenge as we have before."

Mouler still hadn't moved beyond another test of the ground. Toltan could see his hairs rising, no doubt in response to mounting frustration being kept under tight control. He *didn't* know why Mouler didn't put an end to the discussion right then and there. A strong reminder of his place would silence Mesin and his point of view. He never did, and Toltan could not understand why.

"We've lost hunters in challenges before," is all Mouler said. "If these are the same pack that attacked us earlier—"

"Then we should defend our territory!" Mesin said. "We can't let them violate our territory without consequence."

Toltan couldn't stay silent anymore. He swallowed his growl, but his glare was stern and deadly, much like his mother's death stance.

"Fools rush into conflict," he said. "If we are to drive them off, we're better to do so with the full pack. Any less is a risk not worth taking."

Mesin huffed dismissal. "Or a sign of weakness."

"That'll do you two." Mouler said, finally speaking with force. He had turned around and was glaring at them both with his hackles bristling so that even Mesin had to see them.

Toltan dropped his ears at once. Mesin… his demeanor didn't change at all. Why Mouler didn't force them down, again, confused Toltan.

"We will defend our borders once we're fed," Mouler said. "For now, we'll find our kill near the lake. There's always a heard of moose there this time of year. Follow."

Mouler turned for a well known lake at the edge of their territory. If they didn't find larger prey there, smaller kills, including fish, would make up the difference. It was how the pack had grown so large, and Toltan allowed his concern to blow out with a sigh. Mouler had asserted his authority. Now at last they could—

"Mesin!" Mouler again. "Get back here!"

Toltan looked back to see Lavila vanish down the game trail. He didn't need Wolfor's sight to know Mesin was ahead of her. A frustrated growl escaped his control as once again, Mesin's decision making left a lot to be desired, though he'd never defied Mouler before. Yet when the command was repeated, neither wolf came back.

Mouler sprinted down the trail only a short breath before stopping. The rest of the hunting party followed with almost no distance between them. When an alpha runs, you don't ask why, you just follow.

When they stopped however, Toltan did say, "I know he's my brother, but I'm not sure we should save him from this one."

Mouler only growled. He didn't look anywhere, which left Toltan unsure who he was growling at. More to the point, he didn't know what they should do. He'd leave Mesin to whatever fate he'd just brought upon himself. Mouler… all he did was stand there, glaring his own muted death stance down the trail, and no one dared ask or suggest anything further.

All their ears perked as new sounds came from ahead of them. With the wind at their tails, their noses could tell them nothing nor could they see anything. There was only a very quiet grating, much like a growl, that didn't sound like one. It was distant at first, but it grew louder as it approached, and no one could say for sure what it was.

That is until figures appeared in the distance. Just two at first, then more, then a lot more. Instantly, everyone knew *exactly* what it was. It wasn't *a* growl, it was *several*! Mesin had found the wolves on the trail. He and Lavila were using every ounce of their speed not to get caught.

Again, Toltan would have left him to it. Allowing the rival pack to kill Mesin would save the pack so much trouble. He almost suggested they do just that. As the rival pack charged their way, he found the words crawling up his throat with great speed in the hopes of saving the pack from more deaths or injuries brought on by a fool.

Before they got to his mouth, Mouler said loud, firm, and without room for question, "Sound the challenge, and call the pack."

The hunting party lifted their heads in howls. First Mouler's, then the others joined in, all varying their voices to make them sound more numerous than they were. Their pack replied during their howl, also hiding their number while making it clear they were on their way. The other pack did not hesitate nor did they slow, even as the howl was repeated. Whatever Mesin did, it had them so furious they didn't care what they were charging into.

"We shouldn't fight this," Toltan said, surprised at his own burst of courage. "Mesin did this to himself. Let him face the consequences."

"It's too late for that," Mouler said. He was already hunkering down for the coming battle. His ears were forward, his tail and fur high and bristling, and his teeth showing their threat. "He'd lead them to our young. We must make our stand here."

"What of him?"

"I will deal with him later."

Toltan wanted to argue, but he had no time. He barely had enough time to start his own display just as Mesin and Lavila passed him. When they reached the pack, both turned to join their ranks with displays of their own. *At least they're staying to fight.* Except a force Toltan didn't care to count charged right behind them. He didn't dare count, for the number could too easily dull his nerve. They were out-numbered without the rest of the pack. From there, little mattered.

The rival pack hit at full sprint, with Mouler's pack moving only once they were in lunging distance. They engaged as one, fangs and paws clashing en masse. Snarls and yelps echoed off the trees as blood stained both ground and fur, all in a matter of seconds.

Toltan's first opponent was too busy sprinting to think. As such, when the lunge came, his jaws were able to strike with deadly accuracy as he had done before. One bite, straight to the neck, and that was all he needed. His jaws landed right on target to deliver a full mouth bite onto the rival's throat. Toltan's jaws stopped, but his target didn't. Momentum alone tore the wolf's throat open. *One down.*

His second target took more thought, but no less effort.

Eye,

leg,

neck,

CRACK,

next.

The third caught him as he was turning from the kill. Her first bite drew blood from his shoulder. He didn't have time to yelp, only enough to sink his fangs into her neck. He didn't get deep, or a good hold, but he hadn't wanted either. All he needed was enough threat to force her off, which it did when her jaws left his shoulder to defend against his bite. Toltan withdrew, then had to block her fangs with his own as she charged again. As good as he was, this wolf was faster. It only took her three bites to get past him enough to tear a gash on his other shoulder big enough to respect. He tried to retreat, but before he could recover, she went for the kill. The best he could do in time was turn his shoulders so she landed on the back of his neck instead of the throat.

It proved only a marginal improvement, for now she was able to tug, pull, and draw more blood. Though never enough to matter, the word "yet" was attached to that. One's own blood trickling down one's own fur was never a good thing for starters, and he had a lot of that going already. Second, he couldn't get free, nor could he get his jaws on her to force her back. Sooner or later, she'd get him down, and she'd end him. Even if she didn't, the male charging for him would.

The last hunt returned from the depths of Toltan's mind. No, not the hunt. The fight for the kill. He remembered the duel he'd fought as the female that had him now went up, preparing for another hard push, just like the last one. On pure instinct, Toltan collapsed on his side as if fainting. Just like before, his opponent at the same moment pushed down with her full strength. Her body expected his full resistance. Instead it found none.

The force sent her muzzle slamming nose first into the dirt. Something cracked and she fell back yelping great pain while pawing at her muzzle. Toltan couldn't spare any time. He was on his paws faster than he knew he could move. His jaws were on her neck even faster. When they came back, her jugular was still in his mouth.

He dropped it and faced the male… that wasn't there. Just as he'd turned to face him, a flash of smooth silver fur flattened the rival wolf. It sent him rolling into the dirt where Solas appeared to finish what Martol had started.

"Can you fight?" Martol asked, every hair on end and every fang showing.

"Yes," Toltan said.

"Then stay on my tail while we finish this."

Toltan did exactly that. They became a two-wolf team, taking on any who didn't have two or three wolves on them already. With the full pack now in combat, the rival pack was the one horribly outnumbered. It went the same any time they found a target. Martol danced around them, taunting, feinting, and biting useless marks while suffering less. Toltan did the rest, using his lethal aim to maim, blind, or straight kill the target. Between their tandem, and the overwhelming odds in their favor, the rival pack was too out-matched to even run. In no time at all, the yelps faded, as did the growls soon after. The surviving pack scanned the area to make sure no challengers remained.

It wasn't easy. The dead covered the ground. Several victors were tucking a leg, or staining their fur from deep wounds. Toltan had more than a few on his shoulders, though the one didn't feel as deep as he'd thought. He'd likely be fine to hunt by tomorrow, but at least three of his pack mates weren't so lucky.

Toltan allowed a nuzzle for his rescuer. After so much bloodshed, he needed to share the moment with someone, and Martol was available.

"Thank you for the save," he said.

"Happy to help," she replied, though she didn't quite return the nuzzle. "Where did they come from this time?"

"I don't know. Mesin… Mesin did *something*. Next thing we know, he and Lavila are running for their lives, and Mouler…"

Toltan stopped as he realized who he hadn't seen yet. He looked around and still didn't see the mountain of a wolf he desperately needed to see. He checked every body with his eyes, passing over the rivals with ease, feeling a thorn in his chest as he did the same with each pack mate. Then he realized he was looking for the wrong wolf. Jilsina wouldn't have stayed behind, not with such a frantic howl. Nor would she be among the dead. Too much skill coming in too late for that to happen.

So Toltan checked every wolf not dead in search of her. It wasn't long before he found her, head down, likely caring for someone. He instantly ran to her to see if she knew where Mouler was.

Toltan didn't have to ask, for he found him, in the one place he didn't want to.

On his side, fur so covered in blood he couldn't see much grey.

***

To call the mood grim would be an insult. This made grim look like the birth of a new litter.

Four lay dead on the battlefield. Several more were cleaning deep wounds or carrying legs that appeared unlikely to ever heal properly. Some were already breathing their last, the end just hadn't come yet.

Worse yet was Mouler. Granted, much of the blood wasn't his, but his wounds were still serious. His proud march back to the meeting area had fooled all but those who knew him better. Or those, like Martol, who knew from their care how deep his wounds went.

Sense alone kept Toltan from ignoring his own injuries. Though minor despite the pain, they required care all the same. But he didn't want to care for injuries. He didn't want to watch a fifth member drag himself away because he knew death was coming and didn't want their body to threaten the health or morale of the pack. He didn't want to worry about his alpha and father doing the very same. What he wanted to do was snap Mesin in half a hundred times, break every bone in his body, then find some way to make the crows eat him alive. Sadly, ability and desire rarely coincide.

As such, with his injuries still slowing him, the most he could do was give Mesin a straight-eared snarl as he passed by. When Mesin turned to reply, he found a glare that would have put Jilsina's death stance to shame.

Mesin paused, his ears shifted, but his hesitation lasted only a moment.

"You have something to say, say it," Mesin said.

"You deserve to die," Toltan said.

Mesin again hesitated. For a fraction of a second, his ears and tail headed for submission. Were his shoulder not ready to scream the next time he moved, Toltan would have used it to assert himself. A part of him screamed for him to do exactly that. Instead, he held his snarl, to which Mesin recollected himself in his usual, dismissive confidence.

"I acted in the best interests of my pack."

"'Your pack', has lost five..." Toltan glanced to see two more limping into the forest despite protests from other members. "seven, members today, because of you. Several more are injured because of you. *Your alpha,* is fighting for his life, because of *you*!"

"And we will rise, because of me. Our rivals lay dead. If any remain, they are now too few to threaten us. Wolfor has provided. Our pack will grow strong. I will make sure of it."

Once again, his injury stopped Toltan from reducing Mesin to powder. He snapped to his paws for the lunge, but his shoulder screamed too loudly to let him finish it. Even so, Mesin flinched. He would have gone further had Toltan not cringed with a sharp whine. With the threat clearly never coming, despite Toltan's insides demanding that he try anyway, Mesin regained his confidence.

"You should care for yourself Toltan. The pack will need good hunters like you."

Toltan glared death, though not quite a death stance. "What we need, is to be rid of you."

"Not going to happen. Especially now."

He walked off, leaving Toltan growling through his pain.

Toltan barely felt it through the rage. One foolish wolf had caused so much, yet he could do nothing. He wasn't alpha, though he really wanted to be right now. Were he not so injured, he might have put Mesin in his place, or killed him. He couldn't decide which. A part of him still screamed for him to try anyway, but it was ignored.

If only he'd spoken faster. True it would have caused Mesin's death, but two is far better than seven, especially given the two. Okay, Lavila would be missed as a vital tension breaker. Losing Mesin however... hard to not call it a worthy sacrifice.

"He's going to be alpha."

Toltan snapped his head around to find Martol standing behind him. Had she been there the whole time? Had she heard their conversation? Part of him wanted to know. More of him was terrified at her words, her low ears, bloodied muzzle, and worst of all, the lack of doubt within himself.

"He can't," Toltan said, as much to himself as Martol. "Mouler would never allow it."

Martol sounded like she was miles away. "Mouler isn't going to last. And Mesin has few rivals left to him."

"Few," Toltan echoed, rising to his paws despite the pain. He did tuck the one leg however. "All it takes is one."

"No one will stand. Those that would are dead. The rest, though capable, will feel they can't match him. Mesin will be alpha."

"You don't know that."

"I do. Toltan it scares me, but I do. Something in him has changed. Just yesterday, I saw him stand up to Mouler without consequence. There's a fire in him that wasn't there before. One hot enough to burn through most challengers."

Toltan stared at her, trying not to believe her. Trying not to hear his own heart agreeing with her assessment. Yes, Mesin had changed. Even with his moments of fear just a second ago, he could feel a new aura around him. As Martol said, he had a new fire in him. This was not the Mesin who was simply arrogant. This… this was more dangerous, more respectable, more rigid.

Toltan looked back toward the den still trying to deny his instincts. "He doesn't have the blood of an alpha. Surely others will see that."

"None that will stand against him," Martol said. "At least, I don't know of any."

No. Toltan couldn't allow it. He couldn't allow the idea to form. Even the thought made his stomach churn. Mesin as an alpha, Lavila as his mate, a poor pair, neither suited for the role. And yet, who would face him? *Not enough skill, not enough courage, not enough, not enough,* he went through every member in the pack and got the same answer. Even when he asked of himself… it just wasn't there. Yet in his case, the urge was there, yet the "why not" eluded him.

Martol had to be wrong. Mouler would be fine. He'd be down for a while, but that mountain of a wolf couldn't die. He was too stubborn to die. He'd taken on a bear once and come out on top. There's no way…

Toltan's ears perked when he heard whines near the den. His heart stopped cold when he realized it was Jilsina making the sounds. His heart vanished entirely when the sounds he heard were not of physical pain, but of the begging sort. The same kind he'd heard three times already.

Pain or not, Toltan limped as fast as he could toward the den. *A pup has gotten loose, that's all. With so many injured, it would be easy.* He continued to tell himself it wasn't so in every way he could. After all, he would have jumped at the chance at their age. Well, he could catch a few pups. If not him Martol, who was trotting along beside him, careful to stay with him. He liked the company, but was focused on learning the reason for his mother's pain.

He found her, sitting by the den, still as stone. This wasn't a new death stance however. It was a blank look of pain. Were she not whining... he didn't want to think about what that could mean.

Then again, this might be worse. When he looked to see where she was staring, his lungs went wherever his heart had gone. Only a short distance away, a grey mountain of a wolf was limping into the forest.

Toltan allowed a glance at Martol, and found her ears back in pain, yet somehow she was more collected. For her, it was pain only, not even shock. So much so that she soon lifted her head in the long, low howl of mourning. The pack joined in, save for the two wolves beside her.

Jilsina would not move for some time. She would sit there, whining after her mate, praying that somehow he'd come back to her.

Toltan however was too hurt to mourn, and too afraid to move. Mouler, his father, his alpha, was dead. Which meant Martol had been right.

If he wasn't already, Mesin, would be alpha.

Chapter 3

As much as Toltan hated to admit it, Mesin had been right about one thing; the battle had appeared to end the threat of their neighbors.

A hunt along the same game trail just a few days after went so far past the battle ground that they found old territory markings. The key word however was *old.* As in so old they had long ago lost any meaningful scent. If any survived, they weren't policing their borders enough. Mesin of course took the party deeper still to claim more territory for the pack. Thank Wolfor they didn't run into the rest of the rival pack, assuming there were any left.

The hunt itself however was another matter.

A poor choice of target had led to a member getting injured. It was minor and would heal fast, but it shouldn't have happened. Mesin insisted on going for a large buck with antlers as big as he was. "This will feed the whole," he had said. Never mind the smaller doe on the edge of the herd that could barely stand. Toltan could have taken her himself without panting.

Yet when he offered to do so, Mesin's response?

"The pack must eat heartily to sustain itself. We go for my target. Follow."

Toltan was forced to do so, and nearly get killed himself in the attempt. At least Martol had been along for this one. She was able to distract the buck while Toltan used his fangs to land the lethal bite. However, she too ducked under a kick that would have flattened her skull. She probably would have fallen without a sound had it hit.

Toltan thanked Wolfor it hadn't as he ate his part of the kill. Mesin of course choose his parts first, which still made Toltan's stomach war with itself. It needed food, so he ate. The idea of Mesin being alpha made his gut churn, so he really didn't want to.

"We'll find a way," Martol said.

Toltan turned an ear toward her, only then realizing he'd held his latest bite long enough for it to bleed on his jaw. He swallowed it with a quick lick after. "To do what?"

"Survive. Make do. I'm not sure yet."

"Not sure there's anything to be done. He's alpha now."

"He doesn't have to be."

Toltan turned straight-eared at her, more curious than surprised. "You have someone in mind? Mouler was the only one who could tame him."

Martol held her own bite. Much like Toltan had, she seemed to fall into herself, turning still as stone while her mind was elsewhere. Except she didn't stay gone as long. With a sigh, she swallowed her bite and went for more without a word. Her ears flashed back long enough to be a cringe, to which Toltan flicked one of his own.

Too bad, Toltan thought. He'd have given a lot for someone to have an answer, or at least a way to quiet his stomach. He'd give his tail if it meant finding a way to not feel like more could be done. Maybe, Wolfor permitting, such a wolf could help him miss his father a little less too.

Instead he was left with a warring stomach and a void within that was neither pain nor fear. If anything, it was the same sinking feeling he had when, for just a moment, he thought he'd caught the rage plague. He couldn't find a reason, nor could he find a source. Only a deep instinct that was driving him crazy.

Toltan forced food down until even the half that wanted it refused more. He tore off as much as he could for the pack before following Mesin back home. Martol's ears flashed cringe again as they moved, leaving Toltan still trying to find an answer. He couldn't figure out what had her so… conflicted? Hurting? He wasn't even sure what it was. Only that it wouldn't let her ears stay straight.

It wasn't until the kill was being shared among the pack that Toltan felt that void churn. It was as if some wind had blown through him, chilling him through his fur. He couldn't understand why, and his insides were so mixed up he couldn't sift through them enough to think about much else. The jumble almost forced what he'd eaten to come back up. He considered letting it so he could feed the pups, except they were eating full meat now.

Toltan's ears then turned toward the den as panic took hold. He didn't know from where, only that he knew *something* was coming. His ears searched for a reason as his legs wanted desperately to go somewhere, but he didn't let them. He had enough to deal with without getting himself involved in something else. Still the panic grew. He half expected the ground to open up and swallow him. He did rise, but didn't move.

Not until he heard sharp whines of terror in the distance.

Ears went up everywhere. Toltan moved so fast he felt like he was flying. The whines faded, save for one voice that had changed to begging. Jilsina's voice. Worse, it sounded just like it had only a few days ago when she had tried to keep Mouler from walking away from the pack.

Toltan pushed for every ounce of speed toward the cries. They were over before he got there, but the scene was fresh when he did.

Jilsina was on her side, uninjured, but ears flat in pain. Other members of the pack who had been closer stood still as stone, much as Toltan did when he realized what had happened. He'd expected an attack. Another pack, a bear, a mountain lion, some foe threatening the pups.

He'd been half right.

He saw Jilsina's pups, all dead. Killed by strong bites to the neck. They laid there together, no doubt cowering in a mini-pack in futile defense. They hadn't understood what was happening, and standing over them, not the least bit of cringe in his ears, stood Mesin. Their blood on his fangs.

It was rare. Something almost never done. Yet Mesin stood as proof that almost was a far cry from never. As the new alpha, it was his right to choose the course of the pack's bloodline. Jilsina's pups belonged to Mouler, not him. Jilsina wasn't his mate either.

Lavila stood near-by, staring like the pack but unlike them, she still had thought behind her eyes. She swallowed hard, fighting back emotion or her last meal. At least she felt something.

Yet as Toltan looked at her, he cursed himself for being so blind. She was fat with pups soon to be born. So soon in fact she had to have become pregnant before Mouler died. *No wonder Mesin was fighting Mouler so much.* He'd defied his alpha already by getting the omega pregnant without permission. Were he not so horrified by the deed before him, Toltan might have been impressed with his ability to hide it from the pack.

Instead, he could only stare. No, that was the outside. Inside he was cursing himself for not moving sooner. His instincts had said act and he hadn't. Somewhere he knew he'd noticed a change in Lavila, but had done nothing. Part of him said it wouldn't have mattered, but it was silenced by a greater part that told him his body, plus Jilsina's, would have been the difference. Mesin had made the kills, but Toltan's heart took the blame for every dead pup he saw.

It wasn't until Martol spoke that time seemed to move again.

"Mesin, what have you done?"

Mesin didn't look at her, or anyone. "I have sowed the seeds of the next generation. My blood will run with this pack, and we shall rise to—"

"The next generation?! You idiot, you just *killed* the next generation!"

Now Mesin went for her. He pinned her to the ground without warning. He'd always been strong, though Toltan had never seen that much speed before. Yet he held Martol tight, even after her tail tucked with whimpers of surrender. For a moment, Toltan thought he might kill her too. Even when he knew he wouldn't, Toltan's insides still wanted to take Mesin down, flatten him like a bug. He never did. His alpha was asserting his place, and he had no right to interfere.

At last, Mesin released Martol. He stood over her still bristling his hackles. "Do not forget your place." Martol did not move. She only whined. "We must focus on the new for our future. Wolfor will provide. The pack will thrive."

Toltan tried so hard to believe that. He saw only the bodies of

Mouler's pups, his own brothers and sisters, siblings he had failed. He thought of Lavila's litter, coming so late in the year they'd see snow before they made their first kill. The pack would have to carry them, in every way, well into winter.

He saw it all and he knew, Mesin was dead wrong.

***

You have got to be kidding me!

It's all Toltan could think as he dug his claws into the snow. He was certain they were about to break off as they tried to stop what had been a full sprint. Better than losing his head to the three bucks coming for him. These weren't just bucks either. They were mountains! Any one could lead a herd, and he was skidding side first toward *three* of them.

At last his paws found hold. They planted on whatever it was under the snow, thanked it for its help, and pushed with all they had for a leap any direction that wasn't full of antlers. One buck tore clear to the ground where he'd just been, while the other two stayed on his tail. His legs discovered a new top speed as he sprinted away from the death trailing him. The bucks stopped once they were satisfied the threat had been driven off.

That it had. Toltan had been at the lead, but the rest of his hunting party had spent no less energy saving their necks. They were just ahead of him, panting deeply from the long chase that had turned against them.

"I don't... think we're... getting anything... from *that* herd," Solas said between breaths.

Toltan was too spent to reply. Even his glare found no energy to use. His insides weren't helping either.

It had been weeks since they'd had a proper kill. As feared, the late born pups were too young to join the hunts, creating a burden for the pack. Fall was in full swing, and they were barely tasting their first meat. Worse, Mesin had continued to lead poor hunts. Toltan had talked his way into leading one of his own, only to find starved deer long picked clean, or herds guarded by demons like the trio he'd just escaped. He tried not to think about the half dozen or more nursing injuries back with the pack, for it might send him over the edge.

Toltan tried to keep his mind blank while his body put itself back together. He kept his party from going anywhere to let them do the same. If he was in no shape to hunt, they weren't much better.

Oddly enough, they never questioned his choices. When a member suggested they move on, he calmly repeated his order to stay put. The only response was a quick forward tick of the ears, and a choice of a comfy spot to curl up for the time being. Solas was the only one to resist, but even he didn't give much. Every time it happened, Toltan felt a burst of energy run through him. He could tell these wolves trusted him, even if he didn't entirely trust himself. It was as if their confidence in him helped nurture confidence in himself. *If only Mesin could be led as easily, perhaps the forest wouldn't be so ruined.*

Toltan's insides turned again at the thought, and the memories. Mouler had often talked about the importance of targeting the easy targets. The weak, the old, the sick, the injured, these were the prey to be hunted. Mesin however, convinced the pack needed the most they could get, often went for the stronger targets. Perfectly healthy bucks, does without any wear on them, it didn't matter so long as they were big.

Except, the forest was claiming the weak anyway. If other predators weren't getting them, the very reason they were weak did. Often the pack wouldn't find these victims until they'd been picked clean or were too old even for them to eat. The only herds not losing members in such ways were protected as well as the last one. Mesin's inability to see the damage he himself was doing made Toltan sick.

It also lit a fire that somehow erased all wear from his body. A glance at his party had him hopeful they had recovered enough. The panting had stopped, and most were more lounging than sleeping. Perhaps he'd spent more energy than he thought running from the demon trio. In any case, it was time to move.

He rose, shook the snow from his fur, and chose a direction. "Come on. Let's find a herd less well guarded."

"I request a herd guarded by a menacing pair of rabbits," Solas said.

"Why menacing rabbits?"

"Then I can fight something I know won't break anything."

Ruffed laughter went through the group, a welcome change from their day of futility.

"I'll see what I can do," Toltan said.

Toltan led a trot in his chosen direction, and the party followed without word, question, or hesitation. Indeed, for a moment he thought he felt some energy coming from them, trust even. Another nice feeling he wished he could hold onto.

More joy followed when he found a trail full of pus. A little old, but fresh enough to lead to a quality target. Without Mesin around, they could pick the right target for a change. The only thing that would have made it better was if Martol were around to help. She was a fine hunter who always seemed to make the hard kills feel easy, and her company wasn't too bad either. Sadly, they would have to do without her this time.

Toltan's trot grew into a run when blood joined the pus on the trail. His mouth watered at the idea of such a large kill gained with so little effort. Given the scents, they might not have to do anything besides sit and wait for it to die. Either way, the trail promised an easy kill and a good meal.

His heart sank when he found it. It was dead all right. Dead and nearly picked clean. It was more a pile of bones and a little flesh than a carcass. The organs were gone, two legs were missing, even the head was light on remaining meat. They'd get enough to silence their stomachs, but little more.

"Unbelievable," Solas said. "With the right wind, I could smell the blood from our last hunt. The one Bonha broke his leg on."

"I know," Toltan said.

His ears flashed back in pain as he remembered catching hint of this very trail on the wind that day. Mesin of course, refused to listen. Oh they'd gotten a kill. A paltry fawn, barely enough to feed the party, and three injuries from fighting off the parents. And out here, so close a pup could almost be considered safe, was a kill they may not have even needed to make.

"How long?" Solas said. "How long can we last like this? How long before Mesin has us dropping with empty bellies?"

Another member said, "How long before he has us eating each other 'for the sake of the whole'?"

Toltan snapped at the last, as much to silence the rest as just him. The young wolf tucked ear and tail to Toltan, who came close to a death stance of his own.

"Such questions get us nothing," Toltan said. "We may as well finish what's here. If we find a trail we'll follow it, but I don't think the forest is going to give us anything today."

Growls sounded, but none questioned. Slowly, but resigned to their fate, the hunting party licked, picked, and chewed every scrap they could get from what remained. Toltan had to bite off a few from one small hunk of meat untouched. It would do them little good, while it would do the pups back home... *only slightly more,* Toltan thought with a sigh.

He did allow his party to find what marrow they could before they started for the meeting area. In his mind, they'd earned it, not Mesin. He carried his small offering all the way back while praying for a trail that would lead to an easy kill of better size. The only trails he found were mountain lion and their own.

Toltan took his piece directly to Mesin. He dropped it in front of him and left without stopping or even acknowledging his existence.

Mesin's voice stopped him. "Is that all?"

Toltan had to bite hard within to keep his temper in check. He didn't turn for fear of losing that control. "It is."

"There had to be more."

"There wasn't. We found only clean bones, and herds too well guarded to hunt." Now he turned, glaring his anger at his "brother." "We couldn't even feed ourselves properly."

Mesin gave a short growl, and Toltan prepared for his fangs. He almost wanted it for at the moment, he had no intention of backing down.

Lavila appeared between them. Her ears were low, but her tail was relaxed behind her. "We have enough injured to care for. He brought back enough for the pups. That's more than most found today. Wolfor will provide. Let's be grateful for what he's given us today."

Mesin's ears fell in cringe, but so did his hackles. He took the chunk and walked off with Lavila, leaving Toltan unsure if he felt cheated or relieved. He *wanted* the fight. He *wanted* the release. Lavila had denied him both by being the good omega she'd always been. Amazing that even as alpha female, she had somehow retained the role of fight preventer.

Toltan found a soft patch of snow to lay in where he could work with his fur. Something about his escape had left it feeling unsettled, or maybe it was his fur reacting to his insides. They certainly were far from at ease.

"He'll be the end of us."

Toltan snapped his head up to find Jilsina standing there. She'd always been silent, but the pain in her eyes shook the air between them. It was buried deep, but he could see it. He always could.

"We'll find a way," was the only response Toltan could find, and even he knew how hollow it was.

"You can't hide from it that easily, Toltan. You know what this pack needs. It needs a leader. It needs an alpha to fill the void left by Mouler's loss."

Toltan's ears flashed back as his insides twisted again. "Mesin is alpha now."

Jilsina slipped closer to her death stance, but the pain never left. "Mesin is a fool who will learn soon enough what happens when fools take lead. That's assuming you don't act first."

"Act? What do you want me to do?"

"I want you to remember my blood. *Your* blood! The blood of all wolves. The blood of an alpha. Your father didn't give his life for this pack to see it die like this." Toltan wanted to question the use of the word "die", but the words never came. Only painful memories of Mouler. "His blood is your blood, Toltan. You have the ability in you, I've seen it. Use it. Be the wolf, the alpha, we always thought you would be."

No pressure there. Toltan fought with so many parts of himself he couldn't discern the fighters. Thoughts would die before they finished, some before they ever started. Only one element stood clear, though hard to name.

Fear? *No, too weak.*

Terror? *Still not enough.*

Toltan wanted to believe her, but him? Alpha? He'd already failed the previous litter. He still wasn't sure he hadn't failed Mouler too.

Now she wants him to lead the entire pack? Try as he might, he didn't see that ending well.

Even as part of him begged to be heard, Toltan silenced all talk of it within. As for without…

"It's not that simple," he said. "It's not an easy choice."

Jilsina did not move. "No choice is ever easy. That's why so few can carry the burden of being alpha. Mesin isn't built for it, and you see what it's doing. You are. I know you are."

For a second, Toltan felt full conviction in his choice. Even as his insides turned to mush, for that one second, he had no doubt, and he used it.

"I don't. I'm sorry, I'm not ready. I'm not the alpha you think I am."

Before Toltan's insides could change his mind, Jilsina's ears fell. Her eyes closed in deep cringe, long enough to miss Toltan almost reversing course. He silenced whatever he was going to say before it escaped. His stomach voiced its great displeasure, but at least he wasn't hungry anymore.

Jilsina came out of her cringe with a sigh. When she opened her eyes, they held less light than he'd ever seen in them.

"Then the choice will be made for you," she said. "So long as Mesin leads, this pack will crumble until there is nothing left. Think hard on that Toltan. Think hard on what will happen if you do nothing."

She left, paws heavy with emotion, her tail a limp tuft behind her.

Toltan wanted to say… something… anything… he didn't even know what. His mouth wanted to speak words that would comfort her, bring her hope, though none came to mind.

Soft barks drew his attention. He saw the pups… Mesin's pups… playing in the snow. To a trained eye, they too looked under-fed. What's more, he knew most of the others could see it just as he could. The pack had grown so large it required the best to keep it strong. Mesin was not that alpha. No one had died, but the word "yet" was always attached to that.

Toltan knew it, the pack knew it, but no one was willing to say it. What's more, out of so many no one was willing or able to do anything about it. Jilsina wanted *him* to do something. He tried, he thought about it, but him? Lead such a large pack the way Mouler had? Wolfor would laugh himself out of breath at such an idea.

Or so he told himself, even as a sharp wind ruffled his fur. He didn't let himself think about it as he tucked his nose beneath his tail.

Chapter 4

Martol's thick silver fur bristled ahead of him as if it too was excited about the chase. Toltan tried his best to keep pace, but their target was a fast one. Small too. Either a runt or recently born. Which ever it was, the fawn barely counted as a snack.

Then again, considering the state of their bellies, the hunting party was more than willing to take it.

Yet this fawn was proving incredibly fast. Most of the party had already run out of energy. A testament in and of itself, though if Toltan was honest, it was because desperation had made them spend too much too soon. Those with their needs under control remained. Martol was simply faster than all of them.

Perhaps it's just as well. Seeing her fur showing as much excitement as he felt somehow spurred Toltan on to maintain the chase. His legs burned, but the signal never got through the energy. He might not be able to walk for the rest of the day, but he was determined to have a meal before that.

The chase continued. Snow kicked up as if it were dust, tongues flapped with every step. The party held on without losing ground.

Then the fawn found an old log. With one jump worthy of a seasoned adult, it skipped off the log in a sharp angle to the side. Most of the party did more skidding than turning, mostly into each other, as their paws found only snow. Toltan managed to hold his course, but he lost a lot of speed in the process.

Martol never did. As if she knew what was coming, she had turned ahead of the fawn at almost the same second its hooves met the log.

When it landed, she was there to latch her fangs onto its hind leg. The fawn tried to jump away. The act only pulled the leg out of its socket. The fawn thumped onto the ground without making a sound. Martol's jaws were on its neck before the snow had settled. She held there until the fawn breathed its last.

Toltan had slowed further when he saw the fawn fall. He knew it wouldn't escape Martol's jaws. Not once it hit the ground. The only downside was the drop in energy. The strain of the chase hit at once, and Toltan was sure he wouldn't be chasing so much as a stick for weeks.

Growls and grumbles came from behind as the rest of the hunting party caught up with them. Most were nipping at each other over who ran into whom. Seeing them fighting with each other during such a time made Toltan sick, but he was too tired to do anything about it. So he went for his share of the kill instead. He found Martol had already taken the best parts, and was glaring at all of them. Toltan's ears flashed back, not quite submission, but very much uneasiness.

She looked right at him while her glare softened. "*You* have nothing to fear." She then returned to the others. They slowed their approach and all fighting stopped. Hunger drove them forward despite the death Martol was staring at them.

When they approached the kill, Martol grabbed a leg and walked by them as if they didn't exist. The others ignored her to begin their feeding.

Solas however, turned and said, "Martol, it's not like we didn't try."

Martol growled at him without slowing. Toltan ticked his ears forward in approval before claiming his own share of the kill. She was right. Solas had managed to become pack beta. "Try" wasn't enough. More to the point, he had been among the many too eager to pace themselves. Martol had every right to be angry, and every right to claim the best parts of the kill.

The small party made short work of the fawn. Even though none got more than enough to silence their stomachs for the moment, they'd picked the kill clean in minutes. They'd even managed to get less blood on their fur than normal. *Purely perspective* he told himself. Then again, it was a good reminder of their worsening situation.

Even on the walk home, Toltan could feel his body asking for more. Except he knew there wasn't any more. The forest was thin at best. Empty seemed a better word after the last few days. A word more fitting as Toltan saw other hunting parties coming back with little more than rabbits, and precious few at that. His group found a tree to sleep under while Toltan saw Martol arguing with Mesin. Niether's hackles ever really rose, but Toltan knew Martol wasn't using nice words. He also knew the topic, for which he commended her on. *At least someone is giving Mesin the scolding he deserves.*

Worn from the hunt, and trails too cold anyway, Toltan joined his group for a nap. A few others also returning from a hunt did the same. Not a word was said. Not about their weary legs, or lack of blood on their fur. They chose their spot, curled up, and slept. Like Toltan, many would dream of better hunts, or nightmare about starvation.

Toltan was being eaten by a tree when he jerked awake. The group near him had changed some, but that wasn't what had saved him from the nightmare. He saw the gentle face of Martol instead. Her ears were up, but her head was low, looking at him. Well, not him specifically, but his mind cleared enough to guess she had woken him. The question that had him uneasy; was why?

"What's wrong?" is the question he asked.

She rose her head, drawing herself up in pride. "I'm leaving. You've been the best of this pack. If you're willing to take a risk in favor of survival, follow me. It's time we found our own territory."

Toltan's ears went straight up. *A split? Now?* Snow had only been on the ground a few weeks. If things were bad for the pack as a whole, they might be worse for a smaller pack on its own. And yet, after the shock faded, the idea didn't go away.

At least not for him.

"Are you crazy?" A young wolf named Tona said. "Mesin has half the forest marked. Where would you go?"

Martol didn't react at all, except to shift her stare to Tona. "As far as I have to. You lack confidence, fine. Stay here and starve. I won't stand for that. If I am to starve, it will be because of my own failure." Martol focused on Solas and Toltan, though both were asking themselves why. "You'll never find a mate here. The choice is yours. Make it."

Then the choice will be made for you. Think hard on that Toltan. Think hard on what will happen if you do nothing.

Jilsina's words echoed in Toltan's mind as if she were repeating them. He'd refused to make a choice about Mesin. Right or wrong, he was convinced he could do no better. Now a different choice was presenting itself. For a moment that lasted years, Martol stared at him and he asked himself one simple question.

Why not?

It wasn't the usual dismissive kind. This was an honest search for a reason against it. He was looking for an argument to stay where he was and stay in the current situation. The only reason he found was the chance to best Mesin, and he rejected that one immediately. This was Mesin's pack now. Toltan couldn't change that. He also couldn't stay.

He rose to his paws, shook the snow from his fur, and found the rest had done him a lot of good. He was still hungry, but he had energy to burn again. Good thing considering how far they'd have to go to get out of Mesin's territory.

As others also stood, Toltan looked toward the den. His heart crossed the distance to his mother. Jilsina had been suffering as much as the pack, maybe more. Maybe he shouldn't just leave. Or perhaps... perhaps he should get her. Convince her to join them. Her experience would certainly help the new pack.

He thought and considered, but his paws never moved. Somehow, something inside suggested she was better off where she was. He did know a delay would only make it harder for them later. The weather was good, they were fresh and not completely starving. The time was now. If they were to do this, they couldn't wait.

Tona meanwhile flicked an ear before resting his head on his paws. "Fine, go. I hear you make it, *maybe* I'll join you."

Martol ruffed dismissal at him. She turned and led those standing into a trot away from their former pack. As the meeting area fell behind them, Martol glanced back at the new pack behind her. Toltan suspected she was doing the same thing he did a moment later; Taking stock of the new pack. He counted eight total members. Most were young, though some had experience. All were slightly under-fed, but not enough to be serious… yet.

The yet worried Toltan. Martol had assumed leadership of their new group. She'd never led a hunt he'd been on, but he knew she was good at bringing down difficult kills. Perhaps the rest would come.

No choice is ever easy.

Jilsina's voice again echoed in Toltan's mind. This time it seemed to be demanding something of him, though what, he didn't understand.

His thoughts stopped when one of the females, Carfen, went ahead of Martol. She planted herself in front, raised her tail and hackles, and snarled challenge. Toltan didn't know her well beyond her pelt, as she was the only one with so little grey or brown in an otherwise pale coat. He *did* know her skills were little more than decent. No match for Martol. Thus he didn't expect much to come of this challenge, unless she forced the issue. Then he expected Carfen to do a lot of whining very soon.

Carfen barked through her snarl, trying to look more menacing. Martol didn't move. She held her ground, and her snarl, without waiver. Ignore her head, and one might have thought her frozen solid. Carfen shifted uneasily on her paws. Her jaws twitched as if unable to get set. Signs of a weak fighter Martol knew all too well. A fact she proved in her lack of reaction.

Finally, Carfen's display weakened, then fell silent. She dropped her tail, followed by her ears. Her head lowered with a soft whine to complete her surrender. When Martol simply stopped snarling, Carfen retook her place in the group without a word.

Nicely done, Toltan thought. *An easy assertion of position without injury. Maybe this had a chance of working.*

Martol upped the pace, leading a run in a straight line through the forest. They passed Mesin's marker without so much as a turned ear. It no longer mattered to them. That part of the forest belonged to another pack. They wanted forest as yet unclaimed.

Though as the run continued, Toltan knew they needed something else first. His own stomach was starting to complain, and he'd eaten something recently. Not all of the new pack had. He almost said something, except Martol was starting to slow, or even stop, to examine scents. However each one they found was too old to bother following. The run continued for half a day, maybe more, with the same constant result.

As the frequency of old scents grew, Toltan caught Martol glancing at her pack with a soft whine. He didn't know if anyone else saw it, only that the whine betrayed her thoughts. Toltan returned the look with a forward ear tick in the hopes she'd take it as a show of faith.

They were committed. They were going to live or die on their own. Toltan knew that. He also knew the best way to help was to follow with confidence. While his stomach told him they needed food, now, Martol's concern suggested she knew that too. Thus Toltan didn't need to repeat it.

Despite that concern, Martol kept them moving. They continued to check scents as they went, without anyone complaining or raising a single hair in frustration. Even as the sun faded in favor of a bright full moon, they pressed on, constantly searching for something to sink their teeth into.

The group eventually came to a steep hill, which really was more like a short plateau. Not all that high, just too steep to climb up the center. The pack took a moment to catch their breath while Martol searched around the sides. Toltan watched, curious what she had in mind, until he saw her trot further along the face of the hill. She stopped at a point where the hill shallowed to meet the ground they stood on. A ruff had them moving up this side back along her chosen path.

She was just breaking into a run when she stopped cold for no apparent reason. Toltan managed to avoid her. Half the pack didn't. They plowed into her, and each other, collecting into a pile of fur, snow, and whines. Toltan, like the rest of those not in it, saw the mass of wolf parts and were doing a poor job of suppressing a panted laugh. It looked like someone had chopped up a bunch of wolves, then tossed them into a pile with a thin layer of snow on top. Even as his mind touched on the chance of injury, he couldn't help finding humor in it, especially considering their situation.

The humor faded when Martol pulled herself from the pile and growled.

"Pay attention," she said. "You ruined the scent."

"Fresh was it?" Carfen asked, a bit cynical.

"The pus puddle was still wet."

Ears shot up, then noses planted to the ground as the pack started searching for anything left of the trail. You never got a "pus puddle" from small prey. Which meant if they could find it, they'd have their first good kill in over a moon.

Toltan went away from the group. He knew he'd get nothing but wolf there anyway. He dug at fresh dirt just ahead of where Martol had stopped. It wasn't long until he uncovered the smallest drop of pus. He turned to Martol, only to find her half sniffing half trotting down the very same trail. Her nose was as good as his, so he joined the pack at her tail. That and the moose had left a trail of broken branches and scratched bark any wolf could follow.

Any time Martol slowed, Toltan was able to catch bits of the trail himself. His mouth watered as the scent got stronger by the step. Moose. *Old* moose. The only prey that could feed a pack in one kill. The pus from it's infection kept getting fresher as well. Toltan couldn't contain his drooling. He almost didn't feel hungry through the thrill. Soon, no one was sniffing. They followed the swath of disturbed brush almost running. A kill. A fresh, full kill. They couldn't ask for a better start, especially considering what they'd left behind.

The trail of broken branches grew wider. The pack's pace grew faster. Their mouths watered the trees as they passed. Then they found it. A mountain of a moose. Big enough to feed them and their former pack. Antlers and stature suggesting one older than some trees they knew of. Legs shaking like a leaf in a wind storm.

All alone.

No doubt it got left behind by its herd as the infection of its hips grew worse. It could barely stand, much less keep up. The pack quickly surrounded it, fangs wet with drool over such a meal. Toltan and Solas showed those fangs to test how much fight their prey still had. The moose showed his age by ignoring them in favor of

Martol, the leader and biggest threat. He glared his own challenge, but each step saw the whole beast wobble.

Martol didn't bother with the poking. She charged in directly for its neck. The moose lowered its head to hit her. She stopped and dodged, escaping with only small scratches on her flank.

At the same time, Toltan led an attack of his own. He knew from the buck's strike at Martol he was too experienced to attack directly, so he aimed for the softer targets. The pack followed his lead, and orders, without hesitation.

They took nips at the legs to draw blood and damage muscles. Feints too shallow to do any real damage, yet too deep for the moose to ignore. Each attacker was pushed away with well placed antlers but few were touched, fewer drew blood, and none were ever serious. Toltan thought about the hind-quarters, but decided against testing the old moose's aim.

Their distraction also gave Martol another chance. When the moose staggered at another of the pack, she went for the neck. Toltan went for a bite on the opposite side. The moose went for him, and forgot Martol, until it was too late. Age and wounds kept it from moving fast enough. Her jaws sank deep into its neck. The moose tossed his head anyway, only to seal his fate in the process. She was thrown off, taking a chunk of his neck with her. The pack stood back and waited until the moose thundered onto his side. Blood loss claimed him soon after.

The pack didn't wait. Once they were sure of no further resistance, they tore into it as one. The sweet scent of fresh blood from a fresh kill filled their nostrils. Their muzzles got a good coating of blood as well. Martol of course snarled everyone away from the prime parts. As alpha, those were hers. However her display triggered more of the same.

Those that were there had come from various segments of the old hierarchy. Now they all had a chance to change, or reassert, their status. Not a one passed on it. Snarls and snaps were traded from one wolf to another. Bites were given to those who didn't submit right away. At times, one wolf would slink away, only to show the same aggression to the next. Blood spattered the pack as many turned to claim their position while digging for their next bite.

Toltan didn't take long to assert himself. He wasn't sure where it came from, but he felt a surge of confidence, and he used it. Few snarls his way lasted. Any that did got sharp bites, or were pinned. Solas put up the most fight, but when Toltan planted him on his side, he too surrendered. Toltan ate in peace from there, though he watched carefully as the pack sorted itself out. Before any had gotten much to eat, everyone knew their place. Including a young female only just coming into adulthood being chosen as the new omega. As was her station, she ate last, but the kill was so large even she couldn't finish it.

Bellies finally full, the pack cleaned themselves. Playful nips at stubborn blood drops became frequent. Even Toltan was almost giddy as he did the same with Solas. It'd been a long time since they'd had such a full meal. The bright moon filtering through the trees felt like Wolfor was blessing them and their kill. While they'd found only old trails much of the way, they were fresh enough to suggest there might be enough prey to support them.

Martol collected the excitement in a single, long howl. The pack joined in at once, adding their voices to the eerie chorus. Their unified voice echoed among the trees, somehow bleeding back into themselves, which only spurred them to continue. More than a celebration, it was an announcement. They were telling the forest of their presence, and warning other packs of new competition.

Except they never got a reply. Mesin's pack was long behind them, but Toltan had worried about what other packs they might find. Yet, even after another, shorter howl, there were no other wolves to be heard. Not a single voice rose to counter.

It had to be Wolfor. He had led them to a territory untouched by wolves, likely teaming with game unaccustomed to their presence. It wouldn't last, but it didn't have to. They'd be strong and heavy with pup by spring, with all they would need to continue their growth.

"Come on," Martol said, again shaking herself loose. "Let's go back to that hillside. We've earned ourselves a long nap."

The pack followed her, nipping play with each other as if drunk on the kill.

All except Toltan.

He followed at first, but his mind was elsewhere. Martol was an excellent hunter, and she had done well, however... she wasn't right either. He felt bad thinking it, but he also knew he didn't mean it that way. She certainly wasn't Mesin or Lavila. She just didn't have the whole package. She'd charged in too fast on the buck. Not enough thought given to her attack. Old moose or not, she knew better. Toltan however, had kept his cool, directed the rest of the party better. More to the point, *he* had taken command while she recovered from her charge. Then when she turned for the kill, he had seen it and created the opening she used.

Then one thought pushed him over the edge; she alone had made him submit. None in the new pack ever really did. Now, after the hunt, he no longer felt the need. Martol was an excellent wolf, a vital member of the pack, but in that moment, he did not see her as his alpha.

Toltan advanced to stand in front of her, which put a halt to all play. His fierce snarl and bristling fur made it clear; he wasn't playing either. The pack watched as Martol returned his challenge with equal volume.

This time, it was Martol who barked through her snarl to get him to back down. Toltan didn't flinch. He knew he had the better position. She could use her body better, but his bite accuracy was far greater. In a fight, he knew he could beat her. Thus he held his ground, strong in his position.

Martol tried more barks. They worked as well as Carfen's had. Worse, Toltan countered with barks of his own that saw her flinch every time. Her ears tried to stay forward, but every press from Toltan saw them flick back ever so slightly.

Growling disgust, Martol was forced to accept the truth. She dropped her challenge, then hugged the ground with her ears pulling back. Toltan didn't accept that. He needed to make a statement to cement his place as alpha, more for the others than for her. As such, he bit at her, forcing her to roll onto her back. He stood over her and bit at her neck, still growling. Martol tucked her tail and whined as she offered only submission. No resistance to be had.

Satisfied he'd made his point to everyone, Toltan stepped off of her, his tail raised high to further announce his new status.

"Back to the hillside," he said. "It's time we rested."

Martol gave another disgusted growl, which Toltan ruffed at. She slinked down, and he left it at that. Seeing as he was doing exactly what she was going to do, he understood her comment, which is why he didn't do more. The ruff got the appropriate response. He saw no need to do anything more.

As he led the pack to the hillside to sleep, Toltan felt a surge of pride, or maybe validation. He hadn't acted with Mesin. He *had* acted here. Would his inaction have led to another disaster, or worse? He didn't think so. The pack would have been fine under Martol's care. Still, he couldn't help hearing Jilsina's voice one more time.

"His blood is your blood Toltan. You have the ability in you, I've seen it. Use it. Be the wolf, the alpha, we always thought you would be."

If only she could see him now. She'd be so proud, as would Mouler.

Chapter 5

The snow was thick, but Toltan barely felt it. Stiff wind blew in his face, still his body didn't notice a change. It was too busy with the other body next to him.

"You mind?" Martol said. "Hard to search with you on my paws."

His ears flicked back as he gave her some room. That didn't change the feeling.

Two moons since their arrival had still found no trace of competing packs. Better still, the game trails were as busy as he'd thought. While the game was already adapting to their presence, it wasn't keeping them from hunting with ease.

That ease allowed Toltan to admit what he was feeling. Martol had started this hunt, but he was the first one to join it. He'd spent the entire hunt by her side. Well, more like near her, as being next to her drew more of the same comments. Still, he didn't want to be anywhere else. Hers was the only scent that mattered, even as she kept looking for the one his stomach cared about.

His nose was trying, it just couldn't win either. He watched and admired, wondering what it might take to win her heart.

Martol's head snapped forward, suggesting she'd found something. Before Toltan could find the scent or sound that caused it, her body lunged forward into a run. The sudden acts together broke Toltan's trance. He and the pack were hot on her tail, mouths watering as they all expected a fine meal ahead of them. His stomach surged ahead in the battle for control of his attention, if only for the moment.

It, and much of the pack, sighed disappointment when Martol stopped. She'd found a kill, a large buck even, but it wasn't theirs. It was already dead and partially eaten. The air stank of musk aside from the blood of the kill. A smell Toltan knew all too well.

"So much for no competition," he said. "Though I guess I'll take a mountain lion over a rival pack."

"Only if it leaves us alone," Martol said. "We must take care not to be caught out alone. One lion can be a fierce enemy."

Toltan risked a quick rub against her. "We'll be fine. We have the pack. It won't threaten us."

She ignored him completely in favor of the kill. It was still fresh, and the killer was nowhere on the wind. Small as they were, the pack could eat well off the remainder of the meat. Toltan rushed forward with a snarl to remind the pack of his position, but did nothing more. He chose his portion of the kill before the others filtered in to do the same.

As they ate their fill, Toltan's ears flicked up as Solas dropped a piece of choice meat in front of Martol.

"For you, the best I can provide," Solas said.

Toltan couldn't stop a growl, but either Solas didn't notice, or he didn't care. Martol didn't seem to really notice either of them. Her ear turned up to the growl, she ate the offered meat, then returned to her own portion as if nothing had happened.

At least he's no better off than I am. Toltan thought. Clearly he had a rival for Martol's affection. Though the fact that he'd growled at all confirmed what all the warmth and chasing had meant. He wanted her. The snow hadn't even begun to melt, and already Toltan had chosen his mate. He couldn't remember when it had changed from admiration of her skills to desire. Oh, he'd played with her more often. Offered licks and nuzzles when he could sneak them in. Minor stuff. Yet even he was surprised at the sudden need to lay claim to his chosen mate. Especially since he never thought of himself as the jealous type.

Solas didn't push further, which let Toltan eat his share in peace. It also gave the warmth a chance to come back. He didn't try any signs of affection though. He'd been rejected once before. He knew better than to try again.

At least, not right away.

The pack picked the kill nearly to the bone. Blood was cleaned from muzzles, with a few playful nips exchanged between members. The thicker bones were taken to be chewed on, but otherwise the pack was well fed. They headed back for the meeting area ready to sleep off the heavy meal.

Toltan did risk staying close to Martol on the way. But this time he offered her no affection. Not even a look. He just made sure he was closer to her than anyone else. Maybe that would be enough. Maybe she didn't want him to be so obvious. His maybes didn't seem to be working either. She ignored him the entire way, only paying heed as a good subordinate should. Otherwise, he might as well not exist.

When the pack arrived at their meeting area, sleep was abandoned almost immediately. It started when two members started play-fighting over a bone. Oh, the growls sounded real, but when delivered from the ground, the hind-end wagging in the air, no one thought it was anything else. The challenged gave a soft growl, then dashed through the snow with the bone in her jaws, with her challenger panting on her tail. When he caught her, they mostly nipped at each other, traded the weakest of bites, only to begin the chase anew. Other "fights" broke out, which spread through the pack in what became a mass romping around the area.

Martol didn't have a bone, neither did Toltan. That didn't stop him.

He got down on his forelegs to invite play just the same. When she didn't react at all, he feinted toward her. He nipped at her muzzle, trying to get a reaction.

He finally got one. A very swift, very real nip on his nose. Enough to draw a trickle of blood. Toltan yelped more in surprise than pain. He dropped his play in favor of a confused glare.

When she only glared back, he decided to stop sniffing around the bush.

"What?" he said. "What's with you? Aren't you interested?"

"Not yet," she said. "It's too soon. We're still in the fangs of winter. Let the snow melt on its own before you try creating such heat."

Toltan risked rubbing his muzzle against hers, which Martol

again ignored. "But I want you. I want you to be my partner. I see no reason to wait on that."

"But wait you must. I'm not ready. You'll know when I am."

Toltan tried one last attempt. The only thing he thought might work. "I look forward to it. Like a little wild flower, you'll rise and bloom into wonderful beauty, and I'll be here when you do, to take in your sweet scent."

Martol ruffed disgust, though he thought he'd heard a touch of amusement buried beneath. Still, what was he supposed to do? He wanted her as his mate. He'd made his choice. Yet despite his words, he wasn't sure if she would "bloom" like he hoped. What if she didn't? What then? The only other female not his sibling was Carfen. Not a bad choice by any means, but not the one he'd fallen for. He had no doubt they would make a wonderful pair, assuming he could find a way to win her over. If only Jilsina had come with them. He could get the advice he so desperately needed. With her not available, he did the only thing that made sense.

He backed off… some.

He stopped the constant attempts at play, the endless affectionate rubs, and the more overt attempts to win her over. He continued to sleep near her as much as possible, but beyond that, he spent far less time fawning over her than before. It pained him. More so when Solas didn't do the same, though he got the same reactions Toltan had. Then again, Solas' constant failure allowed him to endure it. After all, it meant Solas wasn't doing any better than he was.

Toltan felt the days drag on forever. He could do little else until Martol was "ready". Had Spring forgotten to come? The wait made it feel like it. The only part that helped was one day out of the blue, Martol spent the entire time running with him as if they were mated. She stayed near him of her own accord. Ran with him, hunted beside him, even enjoyed the post-kill nap nestled close against his fur.

Wolfor's fang did it feel good! More than ever he knew he wanted it to be real. Except the lack of other affection made it clear it wasn't. A test at most, or maybe a reward for not pushing so hard. Whatever the reason, he knew it wasn't her being ready. Thus, he didn't dare push it for fear of ending any hope of her ever accepting him.

Solas of course hadn't given up. He'd continued small signs of affection, mostly offering her portions of his choice from a kill. Martol replied the same way every time; She ate the meal, and went on as if nothing had happened. The nudges got little more than polite replies, and the occasional less polite nip. In truth, she'd started spending more time with Toltan, much to his delight, returned affection or not.

Didn't mean he'd won her though. Indeed, he knew full well that she could still reject him, even if she did bloom as he'd said. This was displayed best when, on a different day, she'd spent all of her time running with Solas. No reason given, no suggestion that Toltan had done – or *not* done – anything to cause it. Just like when she'd run with him, it was as if that day she'd decided to run with Solas. A chance Solas used to show her far more affection, as well as a respect and protectiveness Toltan realized he'd been lacking. Any time a male approached, Solas was up and alert just in case he might try something. He watched only, his straight ears and narrowed glare making the message clear; "Bother her, and you answer to me."

Is that what I'm missing? Dose she want that from me? He couldn't help asking, even as Martol never seemed to sleep as deeply near Solas as she had with him. She never once pressed against Solas' fur, but he couldn't help it. He wanted so badly for her to accept him, he couldn't help wondering if Solas had found something he hadn't been doing right.

It dominated his thoughts, even during a late hunt. A long day of running and searching had found only a very small deer for themselves. Little more than a fawn really. Enough for now, but more would be nice. Yet more couldn't be found. No one worried about it. Even in the best of times, there are days prey just isn't there. Their search found them on the banks of the river in their territory. The ice, which had been thick enough to play on since their arrival, had receded to the far bank. The rest was running gently as if a thaw had begun. Odd for that time of year but not unheard of. Whatever the cause, it let the pack drink from the cold waters to help alleviate the strain of the hunt.

During the drink, Carfen jumped back with a yip as if something had bitten her. She drew everyone's ears, but Toltan gave her his full attention. Somewhere in that instant, he saw this as his chance to show Martol a different side of himself.

"What happened?" he asked. "Are you hurt?"

Martol flicked an ear with a soft growl. Toltan ignored it. His heart was too busy being desperate.

Carfen's ears softened the second Toltan came closer to her. "I'm fine. I got my nose slapped by a fish. I didn't expect it."

"That's good. I wouldn't want you hurt. Of course I'd care for you if you were."

"Thank you, Toltan. I appreciate that."

A grumble and a growl echoed from Martol. Toltan again ignored it. In truth, at this point he was committed to the cause, even though the cause was over. There wasn't much more to do except offer Carfen a quick rub along her muzzle.

It wasn't the same. It wasn't bad either. In truth, in that moment Toltan realized if he had to "settle" for Carfen, he'd find a happy bonding. She returned his rub with a similar warmth, though nowhere near the kind potential mates would share. Still, his heart would have a hard time accepting it. Martol was the one he strived for. She was the one he wanted to impress. She was the one he wanted to bond with. If only he could find a way to win her.

As he turned to Martol to... gloat? He wasn't sure. He was going to do something, except she wasn't looking at him. She was too busy staring into the river. At first Toltan tilted his head in confusion. Then he saw her lick drool off her lips. He followed her gaze to the water where huge fish were hovering just below the surface.

She wanted one. That stare couldn't mean anything else. Solas had made a show of giving her meat, but this was one she wanted. For some reason, she didn't want to go get it. So, backed by more desperation, Toltan's heart took control.

Unfortunately, his heart rarely hunted.

He landed right on top of the fish Martol had been staring at. *She has to see this!* his heart said. She saw it all right, as did everyone else.

The pack recoiled from the splash, while Martol's ears had gone straight up in surprise.

Toltan plunged his head into the water, desperate to make good on his act. Desperation, and water, threw off his aim. He missed once. He took a breath. He missed again. The water was running through his fur, seeping into his ears. A drink from water this cold was fine. Having it soak your whole head? Even his thick fur wasn't enough. But he had to do this. He had to win her! He tried, tried, tried. Miss. Miss! *Miss!*

Finally the cold became too much. With a whimper he couldn't stop, he rushed out of the water as fast as he'd gone in. He shook himself dry, then glared at the pack, daring any to laugh. His legs and insides shook from the cold and humiliation.

After a tense moment, Martol finally said, "Males. Just like them to get in over their heads for no reason."

Toltan was too embarrassed to reply. He was too cold to be angry. He just sat there, glaring at them. Martol led the pack back toward the hillside, careful to check with Toltan in regards to his authority, but otherwise without fear.

A soft splash behind him drew Toltan's attention. His day got worse when he saw Solas standing there, only his head wet, with a massive trout flopping in his mouth. Except like Toltan, he wasn't joining the others just yet. He just stood there, ears straight and eyes wide in shock. He stood so long the fish went limp and rolled out of his mouth. Martol never saw it. Indeed, no one other than Toltan had. That alone kept his anger from growing.

"What do I have to do?" Solas said. "What is it going to take to convince her to accept me?"

"I'll tell you when I find out," Toltan said.

Both of them spent several days after brooding. Oddly enough, when they each started trying again, neither one growled at the other.

Chapter 6

Despite his lack of progress with Martol, Toltan's efforts as alpha were a source of immense pride. He'd continued to find good game trails even as they changed in response to the pack's presence. He'd taken great effort to claim as much of the river bank as possible since it too would be a valuable resource. *Though maybe I'll let Solas go after the fish.* He'd followed other trails to large herds big enough to feed their former pack three times over. Yet he'd been careful to find and avoid danger, such as a recently discovered bear den. While the territory was easy to live on, he knew he was making prime use of it. Even when other wolves followed, his pack would have control over the best parts of the area.

If only it were enough for her. He still didn't understand why it wasn't. He'd shown affection, attention, care, and the ability to lead the pack to prosperity. Things he thought any female would want in an alpha male. So what was he missing? Was he missing anything? Was it only a matter of time? He asked the wind. At times he asked Wolfor. So far, no response had come.

The best he could do was more of the same. Beyond his muted signs of affection, he continued to scout for new trails, lay claim to the territory often, and howl warning to any nearby. No reply had yet been heard. For the time being, the area was theirs and theirs alone.

As winter started to fade, Toltan was sure Martol would be getting ready. Carfen would be as well, but she didn't hold his heart. Martol did. But earning that interest in return had remained difficult.

So, he waited. He ran with her, licked her, rubbed her, tried everything he could to let her know he cared. Nowhere near as much as before, but still present as a reminder. Moons passed, the snow started to melt, and still he waited. He had to let her decide when she was ready.

Or as it turned out, wait for nature to force her to.

As the first green started sprouting, a strong scent filled the area. Toltan almost jumped out of his fur with excitement when he found it. Martol had gone into heat. His courting words were coming true… sort of. His wildflower was blooming, and her scent was sweeter than any nectar he'd ever found.

He wasted no time taking advantage of it. The moment the scent found his nose, he moved in to begin another round of affection. He wanted to force it, but he respected her enough to still give her the choice. Though if he was honest, he was ready to do a lot of begging this time.

He never got close.

"Get away from her!"

Solas. His ever constant rival. He stood in Toltan's way, snarling challenge and standing every hair on end. Toltan returned the snarl with a raised tail.

"Stand aside," Toltan said. "She's my mate."

"Wrong! I'm the better hunter. I'm the one she wants."

A part of Toltan wanted to let it go if that really was her choice, but his blood wouldn't allow it. If Martol wouldn't mate with him, he couldn't have another pair in his pack. Not before he'd found his own mate and was sure the game could support such an influx of new blood in the pack.

"That doesn't matter," Toltan said. "You're not alpha of this pack."

Solas raised his own tail. "Prove it."

Both continued their snarled challenge, but Toltan looked past Solas at Martol. He wanted her to break the stalemate. He wanted her to say which one she wanted. Instead she just laid down and waited. The message was painfully clear; If he wanted her, he'd have to win her.

Perhaps this was what he'd been missing. Above all, a female wants to know her young will be protected. Jilsina has lost her protector, and lost her pups because of it. Perhaps Martol wanted to be sure her mate would be there to protect her own pups. There had been no chance for Toltan to show his ability to do so. Now there was, and it would decide who would be her mate at the head of the pack.

So be it. Toltan knew Solas wouldn't back down to a display battle. So, he acted first.

He charged straight into Solas. His fangs went for the neck, hoping for a bite that would bring surrender. Solas recoiled enough to save his neck, but his shoulder took the bite instead. Toltan wanted to hold his bite, force Solas onto his side, except Solas returned with a sharp bite of his own right between his shoulders. The reply had to be respected, thus the two separated. Both were bleeding from their first round, Solas far more than Toltan. Neither had lessened their snarl.

Again, Toltan was the aggressor. He charged in, aiming for Solas' injured shoulder. He hoped to force an advantage. Solas put his fangs in his way, forcing Toltan to change targets. His jaws instead found mostly fur just behind Solas' head. What skin he did find he tore into, drawing more blood. Solas managed to push him off, drawing them both into a fang-to-fang duel.

Paws were jabbing at shoulders in search of leverage. Meanwhile both sets of fangs searched for meaningful hits. Toltan was more accurate, though even he did little more than surface damage. Snarls echoed off the trees as the two combatants traded snaps at each other. At times one would appear to get the advantage, only to have the other slip out of the paw-hold to resume the stalemate.

Then at last, Toltan slipped, literally. In preparation for another thrust, his back paws took his full weight. The ground beneath gave way. It only dropped a claw's length, but it was enough to upset his balance. By pure instinct, Toltan managed to land on his paws. While his under-belly had been kept safe, his back was now open. Solas latched his jaws onto the back of his neck before he could recover. Mostly scruff, thank Wolfor, but it was a hold Toltan couldn't shake from. Solas continued to try and push him down or over. Toltan held his ground, though he knew he couldn't for long. He had to act or risk losing the fight, and at this point, probably his life.

As Solas pushed downward, Toltan once again used what he'd learned from previous fights. A wolf in Solas' position always tried the same thing; push down hard to force the other to fall. It was the norm. An expected tactic often used, that Toltan had an answer for. The first time had been an accident. The second time had been instinct. Now, he was going to do it again on purpose.

When Solas went up for another hard push, Toltan went limp. Solas pushed down expecting to find a full force of resistance. When he found none, the misproportion of force sent Solas' muzzle into the ground with all the force meant for Toltan. He tried to maintain his hold by tucking his head. That only meant his forehead hit the ground instead of his nose. His snarl stopped as the impact sent his head spinning. His hold was lost as well, which Toltan used immediately.

He had fangs on Solas' neck and had him on the ground before his opponent remembered what his own name was. Toltan had a firm and lethal hold, but he didn't use it. Not yet. As thought returned to Solas, he tried for a moment to free himself. Toltan bit harder, crushing his throat more and more. Blood seeped out between Toltan's fangs. Solas tried to snarl, but it came out a wheeze.

Don't make me. Toltan thought. *Don't force me to remove you from my pack.*

Solas still tried to escape. He pawed at Toltan, but he couldn't get enough force to do anything. Toltan slowly increased the pressure, giving him every chance to surrender.

Just as Toltan was sure he'd have to make the kill, it ended. Solas changed all at once. His ears fell, his tail tucked, he didn't have the breath to whine, but the pulled-back corners of his mouth did that for him. Toltan instantly relaxed. Not enough to lose his hold, but enough to let Solas breathe. When he had regained his breath, Solas used it to whine surrender. Toltan held his hold and his snarl a little while longer just to ensure his position was his without question.

When Toltan finally released his rival, Solas didn't move. He maintained his submissive display as if waiting for Toltan to strike again.

It was expected.

It was proper.

It was not what Toltan wanted.

"Get up," he said. Firm, forceful, yet without anger or malice. "I made my point. You needn't cower any more."

Solas moved slower than the sun, watching Toltan for any sign of reprimand. Toltan only watched. No growl to be had. No glare. Even his tail had fallen limp behind him. At last, Solas risked a slow rise to his paws, though his head barely rose. When his eyes finally did, Toltan moved away as if he no longer existed.

He went straight up to Martol, some of him still angry at being forced to fight at all. Oh, he understood why, it just didn't negate the frustration. The rest of him however… was too busy trying to decide if he was hopeful, or ready to snap at her if she rejected him again. She was in heat, he'd done everything to show her he was worthy of her. If it wasn't now, it would never be.

"Satisfied?" It's all he could say through the mix of emotions. In truth, his love for her was stronger, it just couldn't get through the mess inside.

Martol replied with the first truly affectionate lick on his muzzle. This wasn't the simple "you're a good wolf" licks he'd gotten from time to time. This… this was the kind he'd been giving her without reply – not counting nips. As he began nuzzling her head, she pushed forward to rub her full body against his. He returned the affection, trying not to jump out of his fur. He'd wanted to be this close to her for so long. Now he was, and when he felt her soul mix with his, it was everything he expected it to be.

She kept moving forward. Her fur constantly pressed against his. Toltan rubbed and nuzzled, no longer fearful she might bite him away again. No, she at last had accepted him as her mate. Her other half, as she was his. She gave no resistance. Not to his advances, his inquiring sniffs at her rear, and not when he mounted her.

His wildflower had bloomed, and as promised, he was there to take in her sweet scent. The first day of many happy ones he knew were in his… in their, future.

Chapter 7

Toltan dug hard and deep. He knew what he had to do, and he was not about to disappoint. Dirt flew past him in clumps. As he got deeper into the hillside, he had to drag it down the tunnel where he could toss it outside. Starting with an old badger den had made the start easy, but that did not negate the work entailed.

Not that he minded. His young were going to be born in this hole. They would venture down this tunnel when they first saw the world. They would grow, live, and taste their first meat inside this hole he was creating with his own paws. Just thinking about it had him almost playful. The joy filled him with so much energy he could have dug for days without tiring, and if that's what it took to make it perfect, then he was fully prepared to do so. Nothing would be too good for his young.

Assuming their mother approved.

After expanding the end point to allow room for two adults – he was *not* going to be an absent father – and their pups, he came out, shook the dirt from his fur, and stepped aside to let Martol inspect his work.

She slipped inside without a word. Toltan stuck his head inside the hole, but otherwise waited her for to voice her opinion. It had to be perfect. She would tolerate no less. He'd done his best, but was it enough? Would it satisfy her? Would she think it adequate for her pups? *What did I miss? I must have missed something. Maybe dig deeper in, or make the chamber bigger – idiot! It needed to be bigger! No! Two adults plus pups, I made enough room... Did I?*

His thoughts stopped when Martol started coming back out. He slipped out of the way to allow her to emerge. She too gave a quick shake before turning toward him.

She gave his muzzle a soft, loving lick. "It's perfect." *YES!* "Thank you, Toltan. It will do quite nicely."

Internally, Toltan was dancing with Wolfor on the moon. Externally, "Anything for My Little Wildflower. Now you settle in while I find a good place to dig a spare."

"Be safe."

She slipped inside while Toltan pranced away to a pre-chosen spot for a second den. He'd found a massive tree sitting on a hill not far from the main hill side. Well, not exactly a hill, seeing as it was maybe ankle-high in relation to the ground around it. Even so, it would further prevent rain from draining in. Some good digging inside would put the main chamber right under the roots. It made for better wall stability, and provided something for the pups to chew on when their teeth came in.

Toltan barely saw his own work this time. Aside from ensuring he did it as well as the last one, his mind was too busy with the future. A good den, a fantastic territory, a mate who'd only grown closer, a strong pack, if Mouler could only see him now. Could Toltan have done as well with their previous pack? Maybe. The territory wasn't as good. They'd killed the one rival pack, but others still roamed.

Here, he could build his pack in total safety. He could feed them at will without even trying. Okay, neither would last forever, but when it changed, his pack would be a force to be reckoned with. As he pranced back home to share in the day's kill, he realized he could not be happier. Pups on the way, a home they had every chance to thrive in, no wolf could ask for more.

Despite Martol's approval, Toltan checked the den every day to make sure it stayed perfect. Martol thanked him for his concern, but started glaring at him after a moon of constant checking. After a while, he got the message. So he checked every fourth day instead. Strangely, that didn't seem to diminish her glare.

At least things outside were warming up. The last of the snow was long gone, and the river was flowing at its normal, strong pace. It was actually enough to serve as a barrier on that side of their territory. They could cross it if needed, but the current was strong enough that making regular crossings to maintain control wouldn't be worth it. Besides, their current holdings were feeding them just fine.

As Martol got heavy with her litter, Toltan found himself chased out of his own den. He partly expected it. Jilsina had done the same to Mouler. Didn't make it any easier. Martol said it would only be a few short days before he'd be allowed back in. Short was not a word Toltan would have used however.

His mind was so busy he couldn't hunt. It took all of his focus just to check the borders on occasion. He spent the rest of his days pacing back and forth in front of the den. He'd tried to plead his case, to talk his way into being there when they were born. Martol would have none of it. She wouldn't budge, which left him watching shadows move day after day.

That is until one day, while most of the pack was out hunting, he heard it. The smallest of whimpers. It leaked out of the den as if a hair-thin stream of water had rolled into the open. It was so quiet he wasn't sure he'd heard it, until he heard it again. Then there was no question.

The first of the pups were out! He had pups! He was a *father*! He almost rushed in, until he remembered Martol's warning. He knew she'd chase him out, and a female giving birth is the most volatile of all wolves. As the whimpers grew, Toltan could only continue his pacing. Carfen alone sat with him, and she was busy failing to hold in her laughter.

From there it would be a mix of joy and torture. Oh he heard the pups, but pups don't come out all at once. It takes time for a full litter to emerge. A lot of time. Too much for Toltan to sit still for. Each whimper reminded him of what was inside, yet he couldn't go in. Not until Martol let him.

So he'd pace, chase a stick, pace, bite an itch, pace, watch the shadows move, pace, it was enough to make his fur crawl.

A single howl drew his ears up. This was not a member of his pack. It was raw, unrefined, not quite holding a solid tone. Clear signs its owner was very, very young. All the same, Carfen responded as did the pack. Though the pack's hunt had taken them deep into the forest, their chorus filled the air, their voices falling and rising mid-howl, making it sound as if they had far more than they really did. They were warning the intruder that this territory was claimed, and he'd best stay away. Toltan only listened as the young voice repeated his call. A higher pitched voice, coming in as an even wave despite his inexperience. It was a request sent to the owners saying, "I am alone. I have no pack. May I join yours?"

Before the pack could respond again, Toltan gave his own reply. A single, descending tone that held but one message. "Come forth."

He barely knew he'd made the choice. Deep inside, Toltan's mind had done all the thinking. One wolf. Too young to have mastered howling. If he couldn't keep his mate safe from such he didn't deserve her. Even if he couldn't, Carfen was there to make sure this loner posed no threat.

Toltan watched and waited, unaware he'd mostly forgotten his pups. "Mostly" that is, because he had placed his bulk directly in front of the den. Should this loner pose a threat, Toltan would make sure he didn't get so much as a claw inside.

A figure appeared in the distance. It hugged the ground, moving so slowly Toltan sometimes wondered if he was moving at all. Finally, the figure turned into a wolf even younger than his voice had said. Wolfor's fang, he was mostly pup. At most a year old, still wearing the smooth body lines only pups ever have. At least his adult fur had grown in. His under side was mostly white, though black covered his back, neck, shoulders, and top of his head. His face and throat were also white, for a moment reminding Toltan of a raccoon's facial marking.

The young wolf approached with ears flat and tail tucked. At least he understood his place. His eyes never left Toltan, who watched with ears and tail up. Carfen raised her tail as well, but was careful to keep it below Toltan's. Otherwise, she watched in silence as the pup slinked up to Toltan. Even as he did, he kept his distance from the den. Another good sign of his upbringing.

When he stopped and watched Toltan for signals, Toltan's ears ticked forward in approval once more. That said, he kept a growl in his voice as he spoke. "What are you doing here, young one?"

"Please," the wolf said. "my name is Lonate. My parents were killed two full moons ago. I am the last survivor of last year's litter."

Toltan snapped back with a quick snarl. "I asked your business, pup! Not your life story. Why are you here?"

Lonate shook as he looked up at Toltan from the ground. "I'm alone. My parents were trying to form a new pack. What few members we had were also killed. I… I'm just looking for a pack willing to take me in."

"So you have come to ask for permission to run with us."

"Yes. Even if it means being your omega. I just want to belong."

"I see. Carfen? What do you say?"

Carfen approached the young wolf with suspicion in her nose. It tested him for anything and everything it could find. Lonate watched her, but did not move. Eventually, Carfen turned to her alpha.

"There's something he's not sharing," she said.

Lonate shook again as Toltan stared at him. *Yes, there is something hidden there. And yet... there is something else. Something I haven't seen in a long time.* Toltan held his stare, examining every hair the young wolf had. When he found neither madness nor malice, he turned to Carfen.

"Do you think he'd threaten the pups?"

Carfen panted a quick laugh. "Even if he somehow got past you, Martol would snap him in half without having to stand up. By the time he grows enough to pose a risk, we'll know what kind of a wolf he is."

Toltan's ears twitched in thought. He stared at Lonate long and hard. The young wolf continued to look back with careful attention. His tail remained tucked behind him, his eyes open and alert. Toltan looked into those eyes in search of anything suspicious or dangerous. Instead he found... desire. A healthy desire to be accepted. To be loved. To be a part of a whole that wolves are born to be.

Toltan decided whatever it was he had hidden was irrelevant. The pack was small enough that another member would be invaluable. Especially one so young, yet already aware of how he must conduct himself.

Toltan dropped his display, save for the tail which did not fall.

"Lonate, listen closely. You may join us. We just had a new litter born, which means you will be watched carefully. Prove you can be trusted, and you will become a close member of this pack. Betray our trust, and you will face our wrath. Am I clear?"

Lonate's ears went erect, almost masking their forward tick to show his agreement. "As air, Great Alpha."

Toltan allowed an amused ruff. "'Toltan' will be fine, pup. Come. Stand guard with us while we wait for the pack to bring us their catch."

Lonate's ears shot up again. "W-w-what? You want me to... to help protect the den?"

Very, very young. Toltan reminded himself. He dropped his tail to help put the young wolf at ease. "Carfen's right. You wouldn't pose any real threat to myself or my mate. How you conduct yourself will determine where you place in the pack."

"What?... Th-th-thank you! I won't let you down!"

"Don't get too excited. You haven't even met the pack yet."

"I can't wait until I do."

Toltan huffed amusement, then surprised himself by flopping onto his paws in resignation. Lonate had provided a nice distraction, but as the young wolf found out the hard way that Carfen was higher than him in the pecking order, his distraction had done little to settle Toltan's nerves. He could still hear soft whimpers from inside the den, and he still wanted to be there. He had to wonder how long it would be before his mate would let him meet his offspring. Would he meet them when they emerged for their first taste of the world? For all it felt to Toltan, it might as well be years.

He watched the den in silence, barely remembering anyone else was there. The sun moved across the sky all the way to the top of the mountains, with only whimpers to tell Toltan that there were indeed pups inside.

That is until his mate's voice echoed down the tunnel.

"Toltan! Come on inside now."

After waiting for so long, the sudden change of permission didn't hit Toltan right. "Why? Is something wrong?"

"Yes. Their father hasn't met them yet. Now get in here while they're awake enough to feel you."

Once he realized his restriction had been lifted, Toltan didn't waste a second. He was in and gone in a flash of crazed father. He stopped only when he reached the end chamber, first to get his own bearings, second to note where his mate and the pups were. She was laying near the far wall, watching him like a good mother should. The pups themselves looked like a layer of fuzz that was moving as if rats were stirring underneath. A sight as joyous as he'd imagined.

But he went to Martol first, whom he greeted with a gentle nuzzle along her muzzle.

"Took you long enough," she said, a sparkle in her eyes betraying the tease.

Toltan didn't take it that way. "It's not like I had a choice. *You're* the one that's been keeping *me* out."

Martol's sparkle was replaced with a glare. "Toltan, I had to be sure the pups were strong. Weak pups make weak wolves. I can't take any chances with the future of our pack."

Toltan sighed because deep down, he agreed with her. Even now they were fragile. Many pups are lost to infection, injury, a weak heart, the risks would take days to count off. Having an energetic father in the den... well, try as he might to think otherwise, he might be a bit of a risk.

"I'm sorry," he said at last. "I... it's just... this is my first litter. The first pups that are *my* blood. I... I can't stand being apart from them."

Martol ruffed amusement before offering a gentle lick on his muzzle. "You're going to be an amazing father, Toltan. You just need to let their mother take care of them first. Be patient."

Toltan sighed again, then rubbed against her. "I'll try, My Little Wildflower." Toltan looked at the tiny tufts of moist fluff that were his pups. "Can I touch them then?"

"You may, gently. They were only just born after all."

Toltan ticked his ears forward in understanding.

Slowly, carefully, he let his nose examine the first of the litter. Soft whimpers seemed to echo in the den, though Toltan admitted it sounded louder to him than it was. These were *his* pups after all. They could barely crawl, and most were crawling around their mother, some looking for fresh milk. They smelled wet, musty, a little muddy, and better than anything he had ever smelled before.

He searched each pup with his nose, an eye trained on Martol for signs of reprimand. As he got none, he continued his examination. He took in every sweet scent of every pup. They merged with his blood so that he would know, instantly, who they were.

At one point, Toltan blew out his nose when dust got in there with the pups. One of them lifted their heads in search of the new air-flow. Before he could react, Toltan's nose had met the pup's. She wined softly at this new contact, then repeated it for a longer moment.

Feeling the tiny speck of wetness on his nose sent Toltan's insides a flutter. It felt like he could suddenly feel the pup as if she had become a part of his own body. His body from shoulder to hip felt light as air, yet warm like the summer sun breaking through his fur. Deep inside, a small flicker of fire also sprang to life. This tiny morsel of life was his blood. An extension of his pack, his family. If she were to ask for it, the world would be hers. If the world came for her, it would regret the encounter. Toltan leaned in to tap noses once again, so he could feel himself come alive in a way unlike anything he had ever felt.

Other pups seemed to sense the arrival of something new and began crawling toward Toltan. To keep them safe while letting them have their moment, he laid down across from Martol to create a sort of contained area between them. The pups all took turns going back and forth. Toltan touched noses with every one, counting as he relished the warmth and fire within himself, each time.

When he had stopped finding new noses, he looked up at his mate. "Nine?"

She ticked her ears forward. "Nine. I know, I can't believe it either. It's a bitter-sweet thing really."

"Why bitter-sweet?" He knew the answer, but his heart had to hear it first.

"They won't all make it. This many? A new territory? We'll never keep them all."

Toltan leaned over to touch noses with Martol this time. "Don't worry, My Little Wildflower. I'll make sure you have as many as possible. I refuse to have my first litter be a failure."

She could only tick her ears forward in agreement. Toltan knew why, and did not press it. There would be pain ahead, but that was a long time from now. Right now, in this moment, he had nine healthy pups to call his own. A strong foundation for the future of his pack.

He went back to the pups, and cleaned a couple as they approached. One drew his attention as there was something odd in his puppy fuzz.

"Am I crazy," he said, "or does this one have silver in his hackles?"

"You're not crazy," Martol said. "I've never seen it happen before. He's not the only one. This one over here is also a little different than normal for a new-born."

Toltan followed her eyes, and realized that a second pup was indeed different. Except this one had much darker fuzz. Darker than any pup he'd ever seen.

"What do you think it means?" Toltan said.

"I think it means that this one has silver in his hackles, and the other has very dark puppy fuzz. I don't think it means anything, Toltan. They are what Wolfor made them. More than that does not matter."

"I suppose not. Though the silver fuzz somehow reminds me of you."

"Now you're just being cute. Especially since his tail and ears are all from his father. As is his spirit I think. He was the first to move, and has done the most moving since."

Toltan watched said pup with a wry sparkle in his eyes. "We may need to watch him then. I gave my parents lots of trouble when I was young."

Martol ruffed a laugh. "I remember. Your mother nearly went insane trying to keep you under control. I think we can do better. After all, we have the master trouble maker as our alpha."

"Then we are in serious trouble."

Both panted laughter again while giving each other an affectionate nuzzle.

As the pups all went for their mother for more milk, Toltan shifted to lay behind his mate. He let her fur, and her soul, meld with his. They leaned into one another, careful not to disturb the pups, but otherwise sharing the entire den with each other. It was a perfect moment neither wanted to end.

But end it did, and quite abruptly.

"Toltan! We've got trouble out here!"

Carfen's voice. The panic in her voice didn't help.

Toltan rushed outside wondering what danger could have Carfen that worried. There weren't any packs in the area. He didn't know of any other threats that would dare go after a wolf pack.

When he got outside he saw both Carfen and Lonate snarling at the shadows. Both had every hair on end, with Lonate going so far as to raise his tail. Toltan found himself impressed. This young wolf was making a very clear, very serious threat to whatever was out there.

Yet Toltan didn't see anything. He looked in the direction of their display, and saw only the forest beginning to darken with the setting sun. Had it been Lonate, he might have dismissed it. But Carfen didn't get that excited over nothing… ever.

"What's going on?" Toltan asked. "What's out there?"

"Mountain lions," Carfen said.

At first Toltan didn't quite understand. One mountain lion was powerful yes, but it couldn't hope to attack them without risking more injury than was worth it. Then his mind heard her answer again. Mountain lion*s*, plural. He couldn't quite accept the idea, but before he could convince himself it was possible, the wind shifted. A breeze ruffled Toltan's fur, bringing with it the unmistakable scent of big cat, and not just one either. His hackles instantly spiked, followed by his tail and lips. He joined the others in their display, warning the enemy of the threat they faced.

Except it didn't turn them away. Instead the mountain lions emerged, two of them, likely a mated pair. They began to stalk at the edge of the shadows, their eyes trained on the wolves. The defenders held their place, moving only to ensure their fangs were pointed at the enemy. They followed the big cats as they walked back and forth, slow and smooth, watching the wolves as if they were the only thing there.

Toltan knew what was coming. He'd seen it before as a young pup on his first hunt. They were testing the defense, looking for the best way in. Attack was coming, and both sides knew who had the advantage. Their best hope lay in the reaction of the pack, and the hesitation of the cats.

Without dropping a hair, Toltan lifted his head in a howl. A single, higher note rang through the trees, echoed by Carfen and, for the most part, Lonate. *The pup must have lost his pack at a young age to be so out of practice.* Toltan repeated the howl twice, as did the others. It carried on the winds, calling the pack to hurry home. It was a call to defend, for the den needed its entire pack to keep their future safe.

The mountain lions split up to stalk in different directions. Toltan was forced to halt his howl to prepare.

"Both of you with me," he said. "We'll have to focus on one."

"What of the den?" Lonate said.

"With any luck, they'll fight to protect each other and ignore it. It's our only chance. The three of us are no match for their claws. Stand ready. Don't move until I do."

The cats grew further apart, still keeping low to the ground as they searched for their chance. Toltan focused on one, making it appear as if he had forgotten the other completely. Carfen and Lonate did the same, which worked perfectly. The one they watched continued to stalk back and forth, almost prancing at times, while the other made its way closer. Toltan waited. He knew the pounce would be announced. He had an ear listening to the other's movements. He could barely hear them, but barely was enough.

Paw by paw, the second mountain lion grew closer. The other maintained its distraction, possibly fooled into thinking it was succeeding.

Then at last, the second cat made its move.

All at once it sprinted for the den. Toltan heard the heavy steps of the sprint and reacted. In a smooth motion echoed by the others, he turned around, jaws open, ears tucked back against his head, every hair standing on end. This cat was going to end, and he was going to be the one to end it!

The mountain lion dug its paws in to stop, then reared up on its hind legs so it could swipe both forepaws at the approaching wolves. The wolves stopped cold, missing the swipes by the width of a claw. The mountain lion roared as it landed, then roared again in disgust. Toltan lunged forward, only to pull back as another pair of paws swiped at him. They repeated this duel twice, both times trading snarls for a roar, and forcing the big cat to retreat a few steps.

"Keep pushing, don't show fear!" Toltan said.

Both of his pack mates did. Better still, Lonate gave such a snarl that the mountain lion leapt backwards in retreat. The echoing sound, combined with the glare, made him appear as if he were possessed by Wolfor himself. Toltan contemplated having him attack to see if his skills matched the display.

Deciding against it, he told the others to hold their ground while he turned to face the first mountain lion. His heart sank when he realized his plan had backfired. The first mountain lion hadn't come to defend its mate. It had instead been stalking quickly toward the den. He sprinted for all his speed to meet it. He could not, *would not,* allow that mountain lion inside unchallenged.

The big cat ignored him completely. That is until his jaws went for its neck. Then one giant paw swept up and caught him on the side of the head. The claws left only shallow cuts on his neck and around his ear. The force however knocked his sense from him for just a moment. He stumbled to maintain his stance. It was all the mountain lion needed. It slipped past him into the den, untouched, with only Martol to defend.

By the time Toltan's mind had cleared, he had no choice but to duck under the lunging paws of the second mountain lion. It missed, but it had landed between him and the den. He braced for a lunge of his own, using all the panic in him to prepare his legs. If it was the last thing he did, these cats were going to *die.*

The pack pounced first. The entire party landed on the mountain lion as if Wolfor had dropped them there. The cat, too stunned by so many suddenly on it, whirled around, swiping at anything and everything. Yelps sounded as it caught flanks and legs, but the pack's arrival had left it so out-of-sorts it couldn't do any real damage. Meanwhile, the pack was using their full strength. Jaws descended every time claws weren't there. The hindquarters of the mountain lion were almost completely blood in seconds.

The cat tried to defend itself, but damage done quickly left it unable to even turn around anymore. It tried one more time, and instead fell on its side. The pack descended upon it en masse. Eight wolves, driven to frenzy in defense of their young, bit at all the sensitive areas hard, fast, and merciless. The cat's roars turned to caterwauls, but that was all the fight it could offer. So many jaws. So many wolves. So many broken bones. The cat was dead before its cries had stopped echoing off the trees.

Toltan, still bleeding from his head and shoulder, went for the den to save his mate. He instead found the other mountain lion leaving as fast as it could. It's front half was covered in blood. At first Toltan stopped for fear it was the blood of his mate. Then he saw the real source.

The mountain lion had made a fatal mistake; Martol was alone, true, but she had the open end of the den, and she had nine pups that had only just been born. She was high on emotion, high on hormones, and at the sight of an enemy, very, *very*, angry.

In this state, Martol had apparently become a one wolf pack. The mountain lion was already holding a bloody left leg tight against its body. Its right eye was closed shut and bleeding. Its right ear was *missing*. Its good leg still had several points from which blood was flowing. The paw on that leg had deep bite marks on it. The side of its neck had a gash from top to bottom. By the time it emerged from the den, it was in no state to fight. As such, Toltan, still panicked from the thought of losing his mate and pups, introduced the mountain lion to the other one-wolf-pack in the area.

His first strike took out the other eye. The next cracked through every bone in its right wrist. As the cat fell, his jaws went for the neck. He tore it out in chunks, covering his muzzle in its blood as he ended its life then and there.

With the threat over, Toltan went past the bodies into the den. He had to know. Even as he feared the answer, he had to know how much damage had been done. How many pups he'd lost. He sprinted inside, desperate to be wrong. He reached the end of the tunnel… and was on the ground with jaws on his neck before he remembered what happened.

"Toltan!" Martol said after she released him. "Are you crazy? I could have killed you coming in like that!"

Toltan didn't move. He only looked up. He was looking for bodies, or body parts. He found nine bodies. All still moving around and whimpering for… for whatever it is pups that age look for. He was too busy being happy they were alive to care what they wanted.

He cringed in deep relief when he saw his mate was also barely injured. Most of the blood on her face was the mountain lion's. The rest came from the most minor of wounds on her cheeks.

"I'm sorry," he said. "I… I just… I…"

Martol stopped him by rubbing her muzzle against his. As his emotions finally began to calm, all he could do was close his eyes and feel her warmth against him. He ached from the fight. His cuts hurt too. Martol's pin had gotten his head cloudy again, but his pups were alive. His mate was alive. As his mind looked back over the battle, he was sure his pack was alive too. By Wolfor's fur, he'd come out of this better than he'd dared hope.

"I know," Martol said. "I felt the same when I heard the noise from outside."

They shared the rub a while longer before Martol was forced to return to her pups lest they start crawling out of the den. Toltan got to his paws and shook the dust from his fur.

"Are you all right?" he asked.

"I'm fine. Shaken emotionally, but that will pass. What of our pack? How are they?"

"I'll see how they faired."

Toltan left as fast as he'd entered. In truth it would be a little while before he could spend much time in there again. He'd come so close to losing them. The primal fear any parent feels in such a situation, followed by the rage at the cause of that fear, hung in the walls of den and seeped into his fur as if he could still feel it. Both would need to fade before he could feel much else when inside.

He emerged from the den to find the pack caring for each other's wounds. Only one was on his side breathing at all hard. When Toltan went to check, he saw that his injuries were still mostly minor. The worst were on his belly, which often made one think their lungs were cut open despite only minor damage. He'd likely be up and around by sunrise if not sooner. Lonate, bless his young heart, was hard at work keeping the injured wolf calm despite a significant gash on his own shoulder that was making him limp.

Toltan allowed himself to just be there. He didn't say a word. Didn't move. He stood guard at the den, watching as his pack cared for itself. How close he'd come. Wolfor had to be involved. Did he send him Lonate to make the difference? Did he bring the pack home in time? Did he fight with, or through, Martol? Did it matter?

He shook off the question entirely, then went straight for the second most injured member.

"Lonate, you should lay down yourself. Get that cut cared for."

"It's nothing, Alpha," he said simply. "I'll be fine."

"Lonate. I'll *telling* you to lay down. I'm *going* to care for that cut."

Lonate's ears went erect. When Toltan ticked his ears forward to confirm what he'd just said, Lonate dropped his ears and tail. He eased himself onto the ground, whining softly in pain. *The gash must be deeper than I thought.*

Toltan was careful, but diligent in his work. First the blood was cleaned off to get the fur un-matted. Then he licked and sucked at the wound itself. The cat's claws had cut deep, but no real damage was done. Much like the other's wound, its placement meant the pain made it feel far worse. Toltan's work didn't help, though Lonate only whined softly as he did.

The work didn't stop until he was satisfied he'd done all he could. He then left the pup to check on the others. All had received full care. Some were already finding a place to rest from the sprint home, and the fight they found soon after. All were eyeing the dead mountain lions as if trying to decide.

Toltan made the decision for them. He dug his jaws into the side of one mountain lion, going for the best meat that was his right. The pack joined him one by one. Even the one who'd been on his side joined in the feast. They all settled on the same corpse, bonding over the usual reminders of place. A snap here, a snarl there, a stiff reprimand for the omega who forgot her place, it was like any other kill, and exactly what the pack needed.

The only exception was Lonate. Toltan didn't notice at first, but the young hunter was oddly missing from the fray. He was well enough to eat, so where did he go?

Toltan looked around, and found him slinking away from the second corpse. He was about punish him for taking meat that was not his, when he noticed the young wolf was taking the alpha's portion toward the den. He was taking it to Martol. If only Toltan could let him. Sadly, Martol didn't know him yet, and after what just happened, she might not stop herself this time.

"Lonate! Wait!" Toltan said.

Lonate dropped the meat and froze solid. His eyes turned to Toltan as he approached. Even his ears were too afraid to fall. Toltan allowed an amused ruff to form. The fear was good to see, but not necessary this time.

"Relax, young one. I'll go in first and tell her about you. Then you can take the meat in."

Lonate instantly relaxed. Probably just realized he wasn't about to die. "Thank you, Fair Alpha. I will wait."

"Lonate, my name is Toltan. It will do just fine. Wait here. I'll be right back."

Toltan went inside to update his mate on their new member. As he did, he looked back on the young wolf with great confidence. *Young, desperate to please, by Wolfor what a snarl, and a fine addition to the pack.* A sentiment he felt certain Martol would share.

Chapter 8

"I just don't know, Toltan. It seems early."

Toltan understood her concerns. Especially after losing three pups to an illness. No one was sure where it came from, but they'd all gotten it soon after the mountain lion attack. Six came out of it just fine. The other three… it's a hard thing to see wolves so young cold in the den.

"We won't be able to keep them in much longer anyway," Toltan said. "It's time they were exposed to the outside world."

Martol's ears shifted while a whine escaped her. She looked at her den, then over at the other Solas had dug a while back.

"Maybe we should wait for Carfen's litter," she said. "It's not that much longer."

Carfen, once Toltan's second choice, had become Solas' first. Toltan almost drove them both away when he found out they'd mated. But the prey remained plentiful, and the competition so far consisted of a single pack that had begun to howl in the distance. A small one at that. The extra influx of new blood would do the pack good. Especially after Toltan's litter had been cut down so early. Should more be lost, the second litter would maintain the pack's strength.

Though right now, Martol was trying to use it as an excuse.

"They're ready," Toltan said. "It's time they saw more than dirt walls and those that feed them. Don't worry. Lonate will keep them safe. As will we all. Go on now. Bring them out. We'll wait for you."

Martol again whined. Toltan simply nudged her along, telling her again to bring them out. She eventually relented, slipping inside the den to retrieve her pups. The pack sensed what was coming. They were already gathering around the den to form a barrier. Most had been well trained by Toltan's antics as a pup. Nobody was going to slip away this time.

When Martol finally came out, her fur was raised a bit and she was glaring. Toltan didn't need to ask why. *Wonder who Rajor was going after this time.* The pup had been named for his "controlled rage", though Toltan was beginning to wonder if perhaps they had figured him wrong... or worse, better than they thought. A fierce alpha, though often hard on some members, could be a good thing. However, such a wolf could also become a bully with little real good coming out of his aggression. Toltan prayed for the former, while deep inside some part of him feared it was the latter.

Martol came straight to Toltan. She rubbed against him as the pups trickled out of the den behind her. Her warmth pushed his concerns far from his mind. As always, he took great pleasure in feeling her fur against his. *Rajor will be what he will be. Wolfor knows what he's doing.*

Meanwhile, the youngsters were spreading out away from the den. The adults kept watch, but the pups' curiosity kept them in place better than their guards. They all tested the air, looked around the area, tested the air again, and on the cycle went. Typical for a pup's first day out of the den.

"I named another," Martol said. "The one with more black on her tail? I named her Jinta."

Toltan saw the young pup, who seemed to be hovering near the pup with silver in his fuzz. "Jinta," he echoed. "Any reason?"

Martol offered him a whimsical look. "She reminds me of someone."

Toltan's ears flicked back in a moment of pain. Jinta...? *Jilsina.* His mother. If only she could see him now. See how right she'd been. Maybe she could. She wasn't old when they left, but age was starting to catch up with her. That and with the pack under Mesin's care, she may well have perished with other members of the pack.

He tried not to think about it even as he went through his cycle again. Could he have saved the larger pack? Did he do them wrong by leaving? Should he have taken Jilsina with him? As proud as he was of his own current pack, doubt still clung to the edges of his mind.

That is until he saw the tiny pup leap over one of her siblings at a beetle. She missed, but the thrill of the hunt had her tail waving even as her prey escaped. Could he have done more? Maybe. But he'd done enough. Jilsina's blood ran through him, which meant it ran through them. As he watched his pups acclimate to their new surroundings, he thought... no... he *knew*, he'd do well by them. Jilsina... Mouler... they'd both be proud.

He watched little Jinta continue to examine her surroundings with the excitement only pups ever have. Jilsina? Jinta? He had to admit, the pup did have a similar air about her. As if a part of his mother had been reborn in her. Hard to judge at a young age of course, but if accurate, she might challenge him for alpha someday. Either way, as he tossed the name around in his head, he liked it more and more.

"I think it's a perfect name," he said, offering Martol an affectionate rub.

"I'm glad you like it."

Rajor's voice broke through their moment. "Why is it still dark mommy? I thought you said it would be brighter out here."

Martol cringed, and for good reason. Wolves preferred to retain their identity and thus required that their names be used even between pup and parent. But forcing this on younger pups never worked, despite the frustration it often caused.

Toltan rubbed his muzzle against his mate's in comfort. "They're still young, Martol. Be patient."

"I know, I know," Martol said, "but Toltan, you can't say it doesn't bother you."

"Of course it does. Don't worry, My Little Wildflower. They'll learn."

"Mommy! Why is it still dark?"

Both parents glared at Rajor's indignant tone. Toltan went stiff and took his turn to glare at the tuft of fur standing before him. Rajor got the message. His ears, tail, and body tucked into itself in full submission.

"Don't forget your place, Rajor," he said.

The pup offered only a tiny whimper in reply.

As Martol went about answering his question, Toltan watched over the other pups. Most gathered around to hear the answer while others continued to explore. The circle of adults kept them contained, which let Toltan simply watch in joy.

Solas trotted up and sat next to him with a soft laugh panting out. "Guess there's some of Jilsina in *you* too."

Toltan turned his head at him. "Oh? What do you mean?"

"You have her death stance. Exactly the same in every way. I think it bodes well for them. You'll keep them in line."

"But will I help them thrive?"

"If you have to ask, you learned nothing from our fight. Mouler always said you'd make a fine alpha someday." Solas looked right into his eyes to demand his attention. "He was more right than he knew. You carry the blood of an alpha, Toltan. I suspect some of your pups do too. Thrive? They'll *command* this forest when they're grown. And it will be because of you… and Martol."

Solas looked away as if he were suddenly alone. Toltan gave a play growl before nipping at him. Solas gave a pathetic excuse for a cower in response, to which they both panted laughter.

"I can't wait to see what pups *you* bring to adulthood," Toltan said.

"Only the worst I assure you."

Toltan laughed again, then checked over his pups. They were beginning to scatter, though the pup with silver in his fur had his nose in the air as if in a trance. At first Toltan thought he'd caught a scent, except he wasn't sniffing. He was just sitting there, staring into the sky for some reason. When he saw Martol watching him as closely, he went to her in curiosity.

"How long has he been like that?" he asked.

"Since I told them about the stars," Martol said. "I'm not sure why. Something sure has his attention."

Toltan looked up trying to find anything that might hold his interest. "Can't be a bat. They don't hover still enough. I don't see any owls either."

He kept searching the sky without success. He looked back at his pup still confused at what could be holding his attention so strongly. Had he lost something in the sky and was waiting for it to come out? Toltan remembered waiting for a toad to come back out of the river. He didn't yet understand the concept of the river being a realm the toad could navigate far better than he. It might be something similar. Though that thought died when the pup closed his eyes as if… resting? Absorbing? What was he doing?

"Luna."

Lonate's voice shattered all of Toltan's thoughts. He didn't mind, they were giving him a headache. As he recovered, he only then realized that Lonate had taken just as much interest in the young pup as he and Martol had. Yet the young wolf was staring at the pup with an odd reverence. As if he were… what? Wolfor himself?

"What was that?" Toltan asked.

"Look at him," Lonate said. "He's staring at the moon as if it's calling to him. As if *Wolfor* is calling to him."

The parents looked at their pup as he seemed to be coming out of the trance. Toltan realized then that Lonate was right. He'd been staring at the moon the entire time. Odder still, the silver in his hackles was glowing! Not really. Toltan knew enough to realize it was simply a reflection of the moon's glow in the light color of his fur. Although, he'd never seen anyone's pelt catch the light in such a way before. The combination left no doubt in Toltan's mind of one thing.

"Lonate, I think you've just named him," Toltan said.

"I agree," Martol said. "It fits him perfectly."

As the pup came fully out of his trance, Martol and Toltan repeated his name together.

"Luna."

Attention:

The following stories contain spoilers for "Luna, The Lone Wolf".

If you have already read it, then never mind.

Otherwise, just know that you'll learn about key moments through reading these stories.

Love of an Alpha

Prologue

Though the term "alpha" is often used to speak of one being, it is rare to find a pack truly led by only one wolf. The alpha male and female forge a bond that connects their souls, and makes the two stronger than either can be alone.

But, make no mistake. Male or female, an alpha is an alpha for a reason. They are themselves a force to be reckoned with. The bond forged drives both sides, and even when separated, strength can be found in the other half.

Provided, that bond is not torn asunder by the separation.

Chapter 1

Luna pranced a short distance away from me. Exactly where he wanted me.

I should have seen the excited perk in his ears, the fact that his fur wasn't ruffled at all, that his tail was swaying back and forth behind him. It was all there. Yet I was mesmerized by my anger. *Return to being a stuffy thorn-in-the-paw? Not while I'm your mate you wouldn't.* I'd spent so much of the Winter helping him recover from the loss of our pack, the worry of him acutally doing so made me miss the tease in his words.

Though perhaps, I had also gotten lost in the glow of his hackles. The sun was hitting them just right at the time, making their bright silver appear to glow. This "silver sheen", as Martol had called it, was outlined in a tiny smattering of black, and had been one of the things that drew me to him, even as a pup. As I got older, there were other things that made him all the more desireable, but I'd never lost my admiration for his unqiue fur color.

It always seemed a stark contrast to my own pelt too. For him, aside from his back and hackles, it was mostly silver. As for me, darker grey covered my back as it lightened down my flanks. My legs, ears, and the top of my muzzle were a strong brown, while my underside was a soft off-white. A much more complicated pelt compared to his.

Despite his simple fur, his mind was far from simple. In many ways, it was devious, which I had once again forgotten.

"Well, tough luck," Luna said. "You want to prevent it..." he got low on his front paws with a joyful pant. "you'll have to catch me first."

He tore into the forest as if sprinting after a kill. I threw yells and insults I barely remember. My words were pure spite. My tone... pure play. *He played me again! He'll pay for it this time.*

"Get back here you!" I said as I began my chase. "I'm not finished!"

He didn't slow at all. He led a sprint through the forest, with me hot on his tail. We both sent leaves and twigs jumping as we ran, while a bunch of rabbits dashed for their holes. I might have gone after one, except my current chase was too fun to abandon.

Luna began a wide angle turn, as if he might go back the way we came. I'm not sure what he had in mind, but I was intent on ruining his plans. Just for fun.

Then he stopped. For no reason I could understand, Luna stopped running. He was watching something. Prey? That mocking bird? Another wolf? My mind didn't take the time to ask. He'd fooled me for the last time. I didn't care why he'd stopped. I only cared that I had my chance to punish him for his tease!

I tackled him to the ground without any hesitation. I landed my jaws on the back of his neck, play growl vibrating in my throat. I dug deep enough to hold, but there was no real malice there. Once on the ground, I bit at his neck and shoulders with the same lack of harm.

"Tell me you won't go back," I said. "Tell me you'll never become a thorn."

I expected play nips, a soft growl, sad pleas for forgiveness.

I never expected a real growl.

A deep rumble came from Luna's throat that caught me so off guard, for a moment, my mind went blank. Instinct alone had my ears back in apology, though I watched him as if his fur might somehow tell me what I did wrong.

"What did I do?" I said.

"Nothing," he said. "It's this."

He tossed his head at an odd rock. It was very smooth, almost reflective, with small holes in the sides. Those holes were oddly clean, crisp, and uniformed, like some bizzare woodpecker had taken the time to be sure each hole was like the one before. The rock itself didn't seem to be a solid rock either. More like slabs of rock that had formed a den of sorts. It didn't look very sturdy, though when I realized it was the work of the beings Luna's mockingbird had called "humans"... I only got more confused.

I walked up to the odd rock, letting my nose tell me all it could about it. Luna soon joined me in my investigation, though his ears were more out and alert than mine. I found the same scents Luna told me human things had. Sweet, tang, musk, and that sharp, crisp smell apparently their stone things always have. Normal according to Luna, bizarre to me.

"They were here all right," Luna said. "Not that long ago. Scent is too fresh. Never seen anything like this before."

"Could it be one of their dens?" I asked.

"Too small. Barely enough room inside for one, and they never sleep in stone like this. It's always that thin fur stuff."

"So what is... well hello."

I had come to the only open side of the rock. Inside I found a freshly killed rabbit. Especially after passing by such easy hunting, my mouth watered at this fresh kill, ripe for eating.

"Now they're bringing their own caching places?" Luna said. "Can't these humans find anything themselves?"

"Apparently not," I said. "Still, nice opportunity for us. After chasing you, I could do with a snack."

Luna sniffed at the rock again. He tapped his nose on it, as if testing. I watched and waited, wondering what he was thinking.

"Let's find our own," he said. "I don't trust anything human."

I ruffed with a roll of my eyes. *Stubborn thorn-in-the-paw.* "Oh don't be such a pessimist. It's not a thunder stick, and there aren't any humans around. I see no reason we can't take what's there."

"Nothing human is ever good for us. Leave it. We'll find our own."

He turned to leave, and I followed... at first. My stomach really wanted that meat. It was just sitting there too. I saw no reason to avoid it. It's not like the den would collapse. Even if it did, it was too thin to hurt me.

My stomach stopped me. A second later, I gave in, and turned inside for the rabbit. I wanted a snack, and the humans had left it for me.

Luna called after me. "Estrella! Don't! You don't know—"

The moment I was inside, my world changed.

A loud snap and clank rang behind me as the open side suddenly closed. I was trapped! I rammed my body into the newly closed side, but the rock clanged with every attempt. Thin as it was, I couldn't break through.

"You were saying?" Luna said.

I growled at him from within. "Save the lecture for later. Try to push from the outside."

Luna tried, first on the side that had closed, then on every other side. They never budged. I could smell the fear on him as he met failure after failure. He tried pushing, banging, thumping his side against it, he even tried biting at it. Nothing worked. All he did was make a lot of noise as the rock clanged every time. I didn't know my ears could ring so much. That, and feeling his fear, did little for my own. Yet his pressence was the only thing that kept me from going beyond a simple lack of breath.

"It's no use," Luna said. "We can't get through. But there's gotta be a way. We can't.... I can't...."

No you don't. Don't you lose yourself now! I barked at him to snap him out of it before he could.

"Luna! Take a deep breath. Calm yourself. I'm not hurt, so I choose to believe we're okay for the moment."

Even as I said it, I heard humans' barks in the distance. They were a long way off, but in my current state, it didn't matter. If I couldn't get out... no, I couldn't think like that.

And yet I did. I could feel my heart racing in my chest. For a moment, I could swear the space was getting smaller. Try as I might, fear was taking hold.

"Any other statements you'd like to be wrong about?" Luna said.

I growled at him again, even as I started heaving my own panic.

We tried again. He pulled, I pushed, we reversed it. Nothing. We bit at it, clawed at it, Luna even tried kicking it like that demon doe had. All we got was more noise. After a while, Luna started breathing harder. It wasn't just exertion. His heart... I could only imagine.

What I could imagine, was his fate. I was trapped. Given enough time, maybe I'd get free, but we didn't have it. The humans were getting closer. I saw him through the holes, heaving with every breath. I couldn't take it. Dying myself is bad enough. Watching him die too… I couldn't. I couldn't let him. I knew what I had to do, even as it felt like my insides were being ripped out.

"Luna. Look at me," I said. A perfect calm so that he could hear me. So he could hear my last request. He searched the holes until our eyes met. My ears shifted as this grew even harder. I could see his pain, and I knew how much worse it was about to get. "You have to go. Get out of here before they find you."

I'd barely finished my sentence before he snapped at me.

"Not a chance! I lost my pack in the winter. I won't lose you too."

Stubborn... stubborn wolf. We don't get a choice. "There's nothing you can do for me. This is my time."

Tears began to form in my eyes as his breathing grew even deeper. It's a wonder he didn't faint.

"I won't leave you," he said. "You're my mate. I can't live without you."

Unacceptable! "Yes you can! You have to. Dead or alive, I have to know you're out here living."

"I won't be alive. I won't have any reason to fight."

"You will because I say you will. Promise me, Luna. Promise me you won't die. That you will continue to hunt in this forest until you no longer can. Say the words. Swear it. In Wolfor's name, *swear it!*"

I needed it. Even as I faced my end, I couldn't let him join me. The idea of him not living… I couldn't face Wolfor like that. Luna… my mate. I needed him to live. I couldn't die in peace knowing he could have survived. But he had to make the promise. Without it, he'd go soul dead. The final state before a wolf allows themselves to die. He may still, but not for some time. He'd keep Rajor in check until then. That was enough for me.

Didn't make it hurt any less. Fear of facing my fate wasn't going away. On top of that, understanding of the pain he was about to face hit like a fallen tree. It hurt worse than anything I'd ever felt. Yet I stared at him. Even as tears fell for both of us, I begged… I demanded, that he do this for me. That he make this promise for me. I had to have it. I just... I had to.

Luna fought to speak at first. He fought more to breath. Then at last, it came.

"I promise. In... in Wolfor's name I...I swear.... I will survive. I will live."

I pushed my muzzle against the rock. I pushed as hard as I could so that my nose would squeeze through. It hurt, but it was enough. He touched his nose to mine one last time. I felt our souls merge, one last time. I'd be taking a part of him with me, just as he would keep a part of me. I stayed as long as I could, then pulled away.

"Now," I said, "get out of here. Don't make me watch you get killed. Don't you dare let Rajor beat you either. Not ever."

Luna only turned his ears forward in reply.

Rustling sounded from nearby. The humans were here. Luna looked inside one last time, then sprinted off into the forest. As he did, deep down I knew, he would live. Despite the pain that oath brought him, I knew Luna would survive. Probably become a bitter old wolf ten times worse than Carlin, but at least he'd be alive.

As for me, I could only cower inside the rock as the humans crashed their way through the underbrush. *So that's what Luna meant.* These humans apparently had no concept of stealth. Then again, they didn't need it when their prey was trapped in a magic rock.

There were only a few of them. Some of them appeared rather young based on their smooth skin and thin builds. At least, the few I could get a look at through the holes. As they stepped up to the rock, I started growling at them. Warning them of the danger they had trapped in their rock. They didn't seem to care. They all looked at me, barking excitement. One appeared close to howling. *Can humans howl?*

A young female came close to the side, and peered through the holes. She looked right at me, then sprang into some kind of argument with one of the other humans. When she looked back in, her eyes met mine, and I showed her my fangs. How dare she try to pass as an equal! One of the others pulled her back before I could see how much of her face I could catch. *Too bad, I think I might have been able to draw blood. Could have made it clear; they might have me, but I will not be an easy kill.*

After some more barking between them, the other humans slid branches into the sides of the rock. Two stood at each end, then, using the branches, they lifted me, rock and all, off the ground. Can't say I cared for the sensation as they carried me off into the forest, still barking and yipping at each other. The first female seemed to still be arguing with the others, though I couldn't figure out why. Best guess I had was that perhaps she felt she should get first choice of my meat. *That'll be the day.*

A long howl sounded from behind. Luna's howl. A final goodbye for his mate. Tears streamed anew at losing him, and at the thought of the pain he was about to endure. My own heart ached when I realized, he would have no one at all to comfort him when he needed me most.

I gave a howl of my own to match. It was the best I could offer him. I don't know how much escaped the rock, but knowing Luna, he heard the entire howl.

Chapter 2

Luna's right, humans are weird.

After a long trip I'd rather not repeat, I'd been stuck by something through the holes of the rock. Seconds later, I got woozy, then tired like I'd been awake for days, then sleep swallowed me despite my best efforts to fight it off.

When next I awoke, I'd found myself in what looked like some kind of grass land with only a few trees. There was mountain side that went straight up on one side, and more of that tough, human-made spider thread forming a barrier around the rest of it. The two kept me confined to an area so small, I could stand on one side and see everything within.

Outside the spider thread, I could see humans walking on well worn paths. They all just stood there, staring at me. Gawking and barking at me as if my presence was cause for excitement. On some level, I think I'd have rather been eaten.

Further beyond them were more barriers of spider thread. I could only see the insides of a few, but those I could see were stranger than the humans. One had a mountain lion. Another a bear, though of a darker pelt than I'd ever seen. Then another had what looked like a mountain lion, but this one was much bigger, and its pelt was orange with black stripes all over it. In the distance, I could hear calls like no creature I'd ever heard of. Including a roar every now and then I felt more than heard.

Staying here was definitely not an option. I wasn't about to be prey for these humans, or any of those other animals out there. If I was going to die, I'd at least like to be killed by something familiar.

I sniffed at the spider thread, finding the familiar human stink, as well as a few sweet and tangy things I had never smelled before. The ground seemed workable however. With some effort, I might be able to—

"I wouldn't go near that."

I almost forgot about him. My trapped exsistance was shared by another wolf. He was solid black, with white nipping at his chest, and throat. He also had a comfort level of the humans I could not understand, and it'd taken less than a day for my opinion of him to sink below that of an omega. I could find no shred of pride, prowess, or backbone in him. First time I saw him I had only to ruff at him to get him cowering. Despite that, his attitude toward me had been rather aloof, which only made it all worse.

I glared at him, though didn't quite reach a growl yet.

"Why not?" I said. "Is it going to offend the humans?"

"No," he said. "It'll hurt. A lot. See that thin thread sitting by itself? I don't know why, but when you touch it, it hurts. It leaves your body feeling all tingly for a while too. Best leave it alone."

I looked at this thin thread hanging separate from the webbing. I ruffed at it as if I might scare it off, then surrendered my exploration when it failed to flee.

"Thank you," I said.

I found a shady spot under a tree, and flopped my head on my paws. My… I guess the best term is den mate, laid beside me, offering a gentle nudge I didn't let him finish.

"Cheer up will you?" he said. "This place doesn't have to be so bad. Can be kind of nice if you let it."

Wolfor's fang, what did I do to deserve him as a den mate? "I don't plan to be here that long."

"Oh right, right. You're a wild wolf. You belong out there in freedom and endless forest."

I lifted my head so I could see behind his eyes. I found no wolf there.

"Yes," I said. "So do you. It's sad you've forgotten that."

"Oh I haven't forgotten," he said. "But we don't have a choice. We can't get out. There is no prey here. There are no other wolves here. So either we can find a way to enjoy it, or we can sulk until we rot."

"I choose to rot. My mate is out there. I have to return to him."

"This is the zoo. Or so the birds tell me. No one gets out—"

I borrowed one of Luna's tactics. I cut him off before he could finish the thought in the hopes it would shut him up.

"The fact that you're talking to birds says a lot," I said.

He growled frustration, but nothing more. He didn't stay silent either. "You really going to be like this your whole time here? Look around. We're safe, we're always fed, there is reliable water, and you know, the humans can be rather fun at times."

"Until they pull out a thunder stick."

His ears perked while his head tilted. "A what?"

That answers a lot. He'd never been hunted by humans. He'd never seen their power, or been around another wolf who had. He had no fear of them. Nor did he have any wild left in him. A waste of wolf is all he was. Continued conversation would prove just as fruitless.

"Never mind," I said.

I flopped my head back down. I traded stares with humans as they stopped at the webbing. All ages. From pups born just yesterday, to ageing adults too sickly to survive the next hunt. It's a wonder they'd made it that far. Every last one, watching me. Some offering attempts at howls, or in pain, I'm not sure which was which.

I sighed, wishing for a den, or a fresh kill. Anything to make me feel something other than trapped.

My den-mate reached in for a nuzzle. He froze at my growl.

"Really?" he said. "You can't at least be civil? It's bad enough you've never told me your name, now you don't want me near you?"

"Well now, the pup does learn. Very well. My name is Estrella."

"Mine's Darok."

"Darok," I echoed slowly. "Well Darok, let me be clear. I don't want you near me, I don't want to stay here, and I don't plan to have fun with the humans at any point."

He ruffed with a backward turn of his ears. He started to walk away, but stopped to look back.

"You don't have a choice, my dear. There's no way out of here."

"I'll find one. In Wolfor's name, I will be free."

***

Despite my swear, my efforts to escape didn't start well. I finally tested that thin thread, and learned Darok hadn't done the thing justice. My insides didn't feel right for days, which only made the humans force sour water down my throat. That's after they tried to soak my food in the stuff. Like my nose would really miss something with a scent like that.

The mountain side I gave up on within a day. Too steep to climb, too hard to claw through, nothing like any rock I'd ever found. I checked the perimeter several times a day hoping to find any weakness. All I found were more reminders how much that thin spider thread hurt when you touch it.

I don't know when Darok started to grow on me, but as days passed, I found myself being more and more civil with him. I didn't snarl any time he got close, nor did I assert my self as much as I used to. After a full moon of livng together, wither we wanted to or not, I had begun to see him as a packmate. He did have his positive traits. For one thing, he had a better sense of humor than I was used to.

It was through his eyes, that I realized the humans could be rather entertaining. Quite often they would bark at each other for reasons I couldn't figure out, yet somehow, the conversations were amusing. Any time a pup started screaming, their parents would trip over-themselves, sometimes literally, to see what was wrong. It's as if they couldn't recognize a pup's cries for food, or simply attention. And I have never seen any creature fight so hard for one leaf. Any time a human dropped one, assuming it wasn't returned, there would be a quiet sprint between two or three individuals over this one leaf. I never could figure out why. When one of them happened to blow into my tiny territory, my confusion only grew. The leaf was rectangular, with an unnatural vein pattern, and it sure didn't taste like any plant I'd ever run into. Yet these humans seemed to put a great deal of value into it. Even Darok had to admit, the reasoning was beyond him.

Such conversations only renforced his growing charm. I'd even grown to like him enough to play with him. The only thing that still drew a snarl from me was when he tried courting me. I liked him, but not that much. Even if I did, Luna still held that part of my heart. I refused to let him go, no matter what.

Or… so I told myself.

The truth began to creep in like moss growing on a rock. Hope of escape was fading by the day, and even if I did, what then? I knew Luna would try his best to survive, but that didn't mean he had. We'd barely been able to feed ourselves over the Winter. What if he were hurt again, or simply couldn't find a good kill? Or what if a rival pack had driven him off, or worse? For all I knew, Luna was already dead for any reasons not under his control. Which left me wondering; did it matter what I did?

The question didn't get any easier as I exhausted all of my options for escape, however remote. After my second moon there, I found that Darok wasn't the only thing that had grown on me. While I still longed for a much larger territory, not having to scour for food, or hide from danger, did have its advantages. The humans had brought plenty of entertainment with their antics, as well as the occasional random object they filled with amazingly delicious things. As for Darok himself… it's not like I had much choice anymore. Maybe it was time I stopped being so anti-social with him, and start exploring wither or not… wither or not he might do given my lack of choices.

I found myself wondering about that on a day when there weren't many humans around. I was thinking about why I'd been so resistant to the place. It really wasn't so bad, and Darok really was good company once I stopped snarling at him. I'd even started talking to, or at least listening to, some of the birds.

So I wasn't surprised when one landed on the tree above me, and chirped words I could understand. But it was when he repeated them that I realized that this one was different.

And familiar.

"I found you, I found you, I knew I knew I'd find you!"

Darok trotted over as I rose to get a better look at this mocking bird.

"Do I know you little bird?" I said.

"Singing singing I have always been, always always on top of Luna's den."

"On top of..." My ears shot up when I remembered some of the songs I'd heard at his den. The teases, the chirps, the snaps from me and Luna as we tried to shut him up. The laughs we shared after we failed. The voice was the same. Unmistakable. "You're his den bird? What are you doing way out here?"

The bird's song changed from sheer joy, to very deep sorrow.

"Had to find, must restore, since mate go, Luna be sore. Hardly hunt, never howl, had to fix, can't stand his scowl."

Darok stepped, forward tilting his head. "I don't understand. You telling me this Luna is still alive? I thought Estrella said he was a lone wolf."

"Lone wolf he may be, but far more within to see. Promise promise he did give, promise honored he does live!"

Of course he lived. He'd promised he would and by Wolfor, he kept it just like I knew he would. That's not what drowned out Darok's questions for the bird however. The pain came from within. The anger was for me.

How could I let it happen? A few more days, and I might have entertained the idea of mating with this whelp. I was that close to doing what Luna hadn't. That close to letting go of my mate. It didn't matter that I couldn't get to him. I'd refused Rajor for him. I searched for him, forced myself on him, kept him going after the loss of his pack, and now two moons removed, I almost let someone else replace him? I'm not sure who held more of my anger. The humans for doing this to me, or myself for letting it happen.

I growled at no one, then returned to the bird fighting hard to silence it. He didn't deserve my anger. If anything, I owed him more than I could ever repay. Darok stared at me as if I'd scared him. I no doubt was about to. Luna's little bird had brought me more than a reminder.

He'd given me my resolve back.

"Thank you little bird," I said. "You've given me a great deal. Stay close. I'll need you to help me get home."

Darok stepped between us. It took every bit of control I had not to snap him in half. "Hold your tail right there. Have you forgotten where you are? No one leaves the zoo. It's impossible."

"I'll find a way. Luna is still out there. I'm going back to him."

"No, you're not. You can't."

"The humans won't stop me!"

"That's not what I mean, Estrella. You can't go because you belong here, with me."

My ears turned forward while my hackles rose hair by hair. My growl grew just as slowly, until my lips stood on the edge of raising. The mocking bird fluttered off, no doubt avoiding my wrath.

"You did not just say that."

I'll give the whelp credit, he wasn't backing down this time. "Yes I did. Estrella, you're unlike anything I've ever seen."

"That's not saying much."

"You know what I mean! We could have a good life, here, together. No fear, no hunger. We could start our own pack."

"I have a pack. He's waiting for me. No one will stand in my way." I allowed the edge of my fangs to show. "Not even you."

Darok stepped back, more appalled than afraid. "Estrella don't. You don't know what they do to wolves that fight. The last one was taken through the mountain, and never seen again."

I stared at the mountain side with a new hope, and a wild idea. *It can't be that easy.* Surely I hadn't missed the simplest of ways to escape. Did I dare try?

"They'd open the mountain if we fought?" I said.

Darok ticked his ears forward, near frantic. "Then you'd vanish within, and I would never see you again. I don't want that. Estrella, I want you. I need you. I want to be your alpha male."

Solves that problem. I couldn't hide my snarl, nor did I want to. No one tries to replace my Luna. No one.

"You want to be alpha?" I said. "Then show me what you've got."

I lunged at him ,intent on teaching him a lesson. He had so little skill that I was able to easilly knock him up and over onto his back with out any effort. I heard the humans start barking, but that just meant I had their attention. Darok returned to his paws, then charged in full snarl. We traded snaps while pawing at each other. My jaws found legs, shoulder, muzzle, flank. His caught mostly fur. *Must have been born in this place. I've seen pups fight better than this.*

I kept him at a tease. I bit at him, then pulled back and held my snarl. All the while, I kept a close eye on the mountain side. I knew where the opening would come. I just needed it to happen.

My split focus allowed Darok to land a bite on my shoulder just below my neck. This wasn't a disagreement bite either. Had it been better placed, he would have cracked bone. As it was, I could feel blood dampen my fur. This wasn't a test of his skill anymore. He was actually trying to wound me!

I couldn't practice any longer. I snapped his leg bone with one crunch of my jaws. He recoiled with a yelp, though much of his snarl remained. Mine only grew. I didn't let him recover. I charged right into him. I pounded him onto his back again. He tried to paw me away, but he didn't have any idea how. I pushed past and clamped down hard on his neck. Too hard. I felt the break while a quiet snap came from my jaws. When I released my hold, Darok flopped on his side without a sound, his eyes wide in final shock.

I stared at him, trying to refind my breath. *What have I done?* The fight had been planned, but not the kill. He didn't deserve it. A harsh lesson, the cuts, even the broken leg, those were deserved. Not… this. Not an end to a life he didn't mind.

Worse yet, as I looked at his eyes that now saw nothing, I realized that even the fight had been too far. He might not have joined me, but I could have convinced him to help me in my plan, one way or another. Just a harsh act of domminance might have been enough. Instead, I'd gone for him like an intruder… and I'd killed him like one… and he did not deserve either.

By the time I was able to look at anything other than his eyes, I had no time left to check my wounds. A part of the mountain pulled back as I'd seen it do so many times before. Humans appeared in the opening, and I used the ache in my heart to fuel my actions. Before they could get set, I charged right at them, showing them every bloody fang I had. Though in truth, all I felt was sheer panic, and a deep desire to be anywhere but here.

One of the humans ran. The other stood in my way, holding a stick with a vine on the end. His own fear made the stick wobble, making it easy for me to duck under it, and sprint past him into the path behind the mountain. More spider webbing was on the inside on both sides, but ahead of me lay the second whimpering human, and an open path through the webbing.

Not wanting to risk a prolonged fight, I tried to leap past the human. The moment I landed, his paw caught my hind leg. *Big mistake.* Panic, anguish, and instinct sent my jaws driving onto his paw. My bite broke bones beneath, and loosened his grip. The delay allowed his pack-mate to return. He tried to loop the vine over my neck, but I'd seen that before as well. I again ducked under the vine, and exploded out the side of the mountain.

I found myself on the path with humans screaming and running all over the place. A few ran toward me. Too many to fight off even without thunder sticks, and I'd brought enough death for one day. I snarled a challenge at them, but it only slowed them down.

Then a shadow flashed over head.

"Run run, follow follow, this way this way, freedom find!"

I didn't argue. Following a mocking bird was better than any plan I could generate right now. The bird flew through the zoo, and I chased after, dodging humans and several of their rocks they pushed around. Screams followed and preceded me. Those that wanted to get to me couldn't get through those that wanted to get away.

The bird led me past many areas of enclosed spider thread. Forests, grasslands, barren wastelands, a small lake. Each one holding animals I'd never seen before. They were contained, so I focused on the bird and the path ahead.

I could see another mountain range ahead of me. Unlike the one in my territory, these mountains were tall, rusty red, and a flat slate standing straight up. It also ran as far as I could see around the zoo, save for one pass where a mass of humans were. I had no choice. I found the thinnest part of the mass, and charged. The mocking bird fluttered and rasped in the face of some, forcing them to pull back. It proved to be enough. What few reached for me were unable to get a hold. The rest scattered in terror like field mice.

I got into the open, and kept running. I ran down a long path of black colored rock, went over another crossing path of the same rock, and into a pass between two very tall, very smooth, and very square mountains. I followed the narrow path between them until I felt sure I'd lost the humans.

I panted exhaustion worsened by fear. When my thoughts touched on Darok, I suddenly understood what Luna meant when he talked about pinecones in the lungs. It felt like I had two, three, maybe more, lodged in my chest. *Darok didn't deserve that, but he got it all the same. Nothing I can do about it now.* Though the pinecones didn't go away, the thought did get my mind working sooner than before. With the pass opening back up ahead of me, I moved forward in the hopes of getting some idea where I was. All I found was more humans.

They were all walking beside more paths of black rock that had white and yellow stripes running up and down the rock. Massive creatures, much like the ones Luna described to me before, ran along the black rock, always staying between the lines. They all made a soft, wooshing-like growl as they passed, and they ran at speeds I could never dream of matching.

The humans themselves didn't seem to mind those beasts. They kept to the sides of the black rock, except for one path of white lines, which the beasts seemed to let them use every now and then. Otherwise, the humans would go in an out of the square mountains like ants in an anthill.

The more I looked around, the more alien my surroundings were. The air stank of filth, icky taint mixed with sweets, sours, tangs, dirt, and a few other things I couldn't recognize. Some of it was urine and droppings I think, though I couldn't see any of it. I caught a hint of blood from somewhere, but with so much alien scent out there, I'm not so sure it wasn't my own.

Humans were every where. I had no landmark, no familiar trail, nothing at all to work with. I'd lost the bird too, and I didn't dare howl. I had no idea where home was, where I was, or where anything close to safe might be found. For a moment, I felt like the mountains might fall on me any second, as I tried to find anything resembeling anything around me.

Then a young voice came behind me. "You all right there, wolf?"

I snapped around in full snarl and raised hackles, ready to rip whoever it was apart.

A wolf with a mix of grey, black, and silver, immediately dropped his ears and head. "Hey, easy. I'm not your enemy. I didn't find any scent markers, so I'm sorry if I missed one."

I breathed my hackles down and forced my ears back in apology of my own.

"You didn't," I said. "I'm sorry. I'm still shaken up."

The wolf rose, all be it slowly. "For good reason I'm sure. That's a pretty nasty wound you got there. You run into Hitlark?"

"Who?"

"That would be a no. Do yourself a favor. Don't. He's a mean wolf who lives on the other side of town. You'll know his territory. It stinks as much as he does."

"I'll take your word for it."

I retreated back into the pass between the mountains. I found a shaded area, and lay down so I could finally check my wounds. As expected, the one bite was the worst. The rest were superficial cuts that had already stopped bleeding. I began licking them clean, hoping by Wolfor's grace I'd avoid infection.

The other wolf approached, but waited for my invitation before he laid beside me. He watched me care for my wound while I examined him as well.

He was young, probably a year or two behind me at least. The mix of grey, black and silver in his fur blended into an ashy pelt above, however his underside was pure white, leading up his chest to his bottom jaw, as well as the insides of his legs. A rather odd fur coloring for a wolf, but his scent and everything else about him remained consistent. All except for bright blue eyes that clearly weren't impaired, and a tail that for a second, curled over his rear end, and had no black on its tip. I'd heard of wolves that never lost their puppy blue eyes, but never to such an extreme, and even pups never got such a vibrant shade.

"So if it wasn't Hitlark," he said "where'd you get that anyway?"

I stared at him, deciding how much to say. He just looked back with patient ears, waiting to hear my reply. I found no reason to lie, though I did keep my guard up.

"My den mate, for lack of better term," I said.

His head turn was honest, curious, and respecting. "Den mate?"

"We were both trapped inside some kind of spider webbing. He tried to force himself on me. Then he... he said... something that made me think fighting him might lead to my escape."

"I'm guessing it did."

"Yes. But... but I... I wound up killing him in the process. It wasn't my intention, but it happened all the same. After that, the proposed oppening did appear. I then had to evade quite a few humans on my way out of that 'zoo'."

The wolf's ears perked further. "Zoo? You escaped from the zoo? Oh my... I... wow! I've never met anyone who's come out of there. If you don't mind my asking, what's it like in there? I mean, besides the stupid den mate."

Energy like a pup this one. Though he also had some measure of brains as well. He'd listened to my story enough to not only understand, but accurately comment on it. Though Darok didn't deserve what I gave him, he wasn't overly bright either. I wasn't going to punish this young wolf by holding back.

"Torture. At least for me. I was born in the wild. I have a mate out there. The humans caught me. They had me trapped for two moons before I escaped." I looked down the pathway, reminded just how alien this place was. "Now I don't know how to get back to the forests of my home."

The wolf's eyes started glowing from within. "Forest? You live in a forest? A *wild* forest?"

I tilted my head, wondering if he'd lost his mind. "Yes."

"What is it like? What's there?"

"The forest." I said as if he should know, which being a wolf, he should. "Mice and rabbits and deer to hunt, other wolves, mountain lions to fear. A calm, yet proud river, running through it with fish, if you have the wits to catch one, and...are you all right?"

The glow grew with each thing I mentioned. When the river came up, he looked like a pup begging for his first meat. I debated pinning him like one before he injured me further in his excitement.

"Think there's room for someone like me there?" He said.

I don't know. Are you always like this? "Possibly. Why do you care? Don't you live here?"

"I don't want to. There are too many humans, and the place stinks worse than a skunk. I want the wild. Ever since my mom died,

I've wanted to live free from this place. Live where it's just me, my prey, and my pack. I've just never had a place to go. Now I do." He stopped. His ears pulled back in submission. "Please, wolf. Let me come with you. I don't care if I'm your omega. I just want to be anywhere but here."

Somehow, despite his enthusiasm, I couldn't see him becoming an omega. Even if he were, Luna and I could use another set of fangs to help with hunts. I didn't need long to think before I made my decision. Luna would just have to deal with it.

Assuming I could find him. More thinking reminded me of one problem I had to fix first.

"Company would be nice to have on the journey," I said. "I doubt Luna would mind you too much either. But it's a moot point. I don't know where home is. I have no idea how to get there."

"Follow follow stay with me, home to Luna you'll soon be. Travel long to setting sun, in your home you will soon run."

I looked up to find the little mocking bird perched on the mountain side. Never thought I'd be so glad to hear him.

The young wolf stared at the bird for a moment before he returned to me. "You know him?"

The bird chirped before I could answer. "Moons, days, seasons go. Estre… Est… Est..rell..lla… Luna mate I long will know."

I couldn't help laughing at him as he fought to keep his song going. Too bad Luna wasn't there. He'd have loved it.

So I made the snide comment for him.

"Just can't get my name to fit your rhythm can you? What's wrong? Cat got your tongue?"

The bird rasped at me before fluttering off. I panted laughter again, as did the young wolf.

"I think you offended him," he said.

My ears turned forward, still panting. "Probably. Luna would be thrilled."

"Yes. Luna. You know, I know more about this mate of yours than I do about you. By Wolfor, I don't even know your name."

"I don't know yours either." He gave my a dirty look, till a nudge from me got his ears perking. "Estrella. My name is Estrella."

His ears still hadn't softened, though his voice sure did. "Tilhack."

"Nice to meet you, Tilhack. Now come, we have a long way to go."

I shook stiffness from my body, and returned to the edge of the pass. With midday already past, I got a perfect bearing on where the sun set. "Into the setting sun", as the bird put it. Getting past the humans proved to be a much larger challenge.

Tilhack returned to my side, and followed my stare at the mass of humans out there.

"I wouldn't chance it," he said. "Not yet anyway. One thing you learn around here, is you never let yourself be seen in the daytime. Not if you can help it."

I breathed anger while trying to tell myself he was wrong. "We can't just sit here."

"On the contrary my dear wolf. That's exactly what we're going to do. The humans almost never come back here."

I looked back the way I'd come, and noticed there was a lot more to this pass than I'd seen in my sprint. *I ran farther than I thought.* While I could see it from where I stood, the other end of the pass was still a short sprint away. Just enough territory for a small pack to use. There were some strange boulders nearby that stank of decaying meats and plants, and other things I didn't want to think about. Tiny streams of water converged in the middle of splitting paths, where it vanished into holes in the ground into an underground lake of some sort. I didn't much care for the smell of that water, but it was water all the same. Despite the problems of it, this small area held cover, and scents that suggested prey could be found here. As well as scraps that, if careful, could sustain me.

"Not sure why they don't," I said. "It's not my first choice, but if you live here, the territory can't be that bad."

Tilhack flicked an ear like he didn't really agree. "It works. As for the humans, they hate it. I can smell the fear on them every time I see them. Maybe they fear us, or they hate the smell despite dumping their scraps back here, I don't know."

"Think it'll keep the humans from the zoo from finding me?"

"For a while. We're probably good for today. We'll leave the city tonight when most of the humans are gone."

"The city?"

"You really are a wild wolf aren't you?" Tilhack tossed his head at the mass of humans and beasts in front of us. "That's the city. This place is the city. It's not a good place for creatures of the wild."

I went deeper into the pass for better cover with a huff. "You seem to do all right."

Tilhack followed, hesitant only in his words. "I... I'm better adapted to this place. I understand it better. I saw you sprint across the black rock. You're lucky one of those beasts didn't run you over. I find a lot of my meals that way. You don't have a chance against those things."

I couldn't argue with that. Anything that big would be more than I could handle for sure.

I looked around still feeling trapped in an odd way. What I wouldn't give for a tree, or something even remotely close to home. This city... I didn't belong here. Yet I couldn't just leave.

Tilhack rubbed his muzzle against my uninjured shoulder to get my attention. "Come on. There's a place we can rest where the humans won't see us. You look like you could do with a nap, and if you'll let me, I'll see what I can do about that wound."

"I think I'd like that," I said. "Just watch yourself. I already had to teach one wolf a lesson today. I'd rather not make it two."

"Estrella, if there's one thing I already know about you, it's that arguments with you are best avoided. I'll be providing care, nothing more."

Where have you been all my life?

"Do me a favor. When we find Luna, make sure you rub off on him. He could do with some of your wisdom."

Tilhack's ears flashed back. I couldn't quite tell why. I think it was a cringe, but he silenced it before I could get a good look. Afterward, he remained friendly, and very gentle when working with my fur. Still, I couldn't quite relax around him. Something about those eyes didn't sit right with me. Unlike Darok, the issue was about the eyes themselves, not the wolf behind them.

I couldn't find a reason. Nor could I ignore the feeling that there was something different about him. Something that might pose a threat if not watched.

Chapter 3

Getting out of the city turned out to be a breeze after dark. Even though the sides of the mountains were lit by the human's sun-beams, there were too few humans around to pose much of a threat. The black rock seemed empty compared to the daytime, allowing us to use it as needed to avoid being seen.

In fact, we used one path of it to guide us away from the human's mountains, until there was nothing but rolling hills and the black rock to deal with. There were some trees, but those along the black rock had no leaves, and what branches they had were at the top only. Constant threads of thick spider web lay in perfect lines from tree to tree. I didn't want to think about what I'd do if I met the spinner of that thread.

We never found any spider. Humans weren't seen much either. The farther we traveled, the fewer human mountains and black rock we saw. The great beasts had thinned out as well.

I didn't let that lessen my guard. We had more wild to use, and we used it. Endless grass lands that stood taller than I did provided excellent cover. Normal trees were scattered, if there at all, but we used them when we had them. The horizon offered nothing but more of the same as far as I could see. At least it allowed us to see what lay ahead. When we didn't have grass to hide in, we stayed far away from any black rock paths or human mountains, though the few we saw were more like giant boulders. Oddly shaped ones perhaps, but still clearly changed by the humans.

Tilhack was always first to notice. He'd be following the mocking bird, when he was there anyway, only to stop for no apparent reason. He'd look around, test the air, then toss his head to indicate a change of path. I'd fought him the first few times, to which he had some version of the same answer.

"We'll find humans that way. This way should be clear. Trust me, wolf. I know what I'm doing."

I didn't have a good reason to challenge him, so I allowed the change. Minutes later, I'd see in the distance another human den just to the side of a black rock path. Right along the course we had been walking on. After a while, I stopped doubting. I was never disappointed.

He did it again just after sunrise after several days of travel. We hadn't seen a human or their rock beasts since two nights before. Once again, he stopped, tested the air, and looked around the area. This time though, he stepped forward out of the thick grass we'd been using. His ears and eyes were searching forward as if something lay waiting for him. I followed, trying as I had before to catch whatever scent he'd found on the wind. Grass pollen, tree sap, dirt, something similar to moose droppings. Nothing to suggest humans.

Yet Tilhack stood just outside our cover with a sigh and a growl.

"Farmland. Just what we need."

I followed his gaze into the land ahead. Seemed to be the same, except trees and other plants appeared to be growing in perfect rows in square patches. Even a forest of bushy trees that hugged the ground was in the same uniformed pattern. Amid them all were more human boulders. I heard other sounds from within, though the only one I could recognize was barks similar to the dogs that hunted with the humans.

"We made our way through a city," I said. "Surely this farmland isn't that much worse."

Tilhack looked ready to scold me. Instead his ears flashed back. Not just to say no either. "I keep forgetting how different we are. Farmland is far more dangerous. There's not as much cover, the humans have dogs to help protect their territory, and the humans themselves have thunder sticks. Trust me when I say, we'd be better off if it *was* the city."

I had my opening. He'd used the words himself. "How different we are." I'd never stopped trying to understand why those eyes of his bothered me so much. Why the pureness of his white underside didn't look natural. Why, after our time together, I realized he didn't smell quite right for a wolf his age.

Now was my chance to see if I could find some answers.

"Tilhack," I said. "what do you mean when you say we're different? Different how?"

He stared at me for a long time. So long I wasn't sure if he was going to attack or run. His ears never stopped shifting as if they, like his mind, couldn't decide on something. I waited him out. Luna had given me plenty of practice in waiting for my answer.

Tilhack turned back to the farmland as if nothing had happened.

"We should keep moving. We'll see if we can find a way around the farmland. We may need to—"

You're not getting off that easy.

"Tilhack! Don't you change the subject on me. What's so different about us?"

Tilhack ruffed a breath at me. His glare said growl, but his ears said whine. "Well, Dear Wolf, you're from the wild and I was born in the city. That's all."

Wolf. He used it like a name only I carried. It only spawned new questions I needed answers to.

"Tilhack, I know that look. Luna had it too often for me to miss. You're hiding—"

Tilhack glared at me, though never growled. "Do you think of anything else?"

I recoiled, trying to understand the question, as well as the sharp way it was asked. He continued when I couldn't find an answer of my own. "I know he's your mate, but quite frankly I'm getting sick of hearing about this Luna. You talk as if he's here, while you continue to ignore me."

I recoiled again, then tilted my head at him. "Ignore you? What are you talking about?"

"I… never mind. I shouldn't have said anything. Come on."

He trotted ahead before I could say anything. He kept moving at too fast a pace to make him stop so I could try again. Not without making more noise than I was willing to risk. I growled frustration, but followed as he sniffed at more spider thread forming a barrier around the ordered plants. He tapped his nose on it, then hummed.

"No magic. That makes this part easier. Now, we just need to find...."

He paced along the spider thread as it was wound around short, stiff, tree shoots in the ground. The threads kept a constant barrier, and he followed it, glancing at each shoot as he passed them by. I was about ready to risk the noise of asking why when he stopped at one. He sniffed at it, then looked within the barrier with a steady gaze born of experience. He was looking for something specific.

I don't know if he found it. What I do know is he pawed at the shoot, and was able to move it just out of the ground.

"They always miss one." He looked to me much as my parents did before my first hunt. Eyes boring into me as if they might infuse the lesson into me, ears alert for any sign I wouldn't listen. I remember when my sister proved she hadn't heard a word. I doubt Tilhack would be as fierce, but no one invites a reprimand this close to danger. Saving it for later however, was always a possibility.

"Watch your eyes and ears," he said. "This thread can get caught on them, do some serious damage. Once inside, keep your ears perked. You hear a bark, you follow me, and do not question my path. One false step will get us both killed."

I could swallow enough pride to signal agreement for the time being. Let him get away without an answer or two, not so much.

"How do you know all this?" I said.

He didn't even blink. "Let's just say I have a unique perspective."

"That's not an answer."

"It's all you're getting, Wolf. I'm not saying more. Come on."

He pushed under the thread, forcing the tree shoot to slide against the middle of his back with little more than a gentle rattle in complaint. He turned inside to stare at me.

"Well? You coming or not?"

I growled at him, but did as he had to push under the spider thread. I could feel parts of it tug at my fur, but it never dug within. I kept my ears tucked back to be sure they weren't caught as well.

I shook the tickle off my fur, and was forced to follow Tilhack as he moved through the straight forest of trees. Unlike the tall trunks of home, these were more like massive bushes, and were spotted with some kind of orange fruit. Sour smelling ones at that.

"Remind me not to dig a den here," I said, trying to sneeze the scent out of my head.

Tilhack only ruffed a chuckle from ahead. "That's why we're here. These trees should hide our scent."

"From what? The humans? Their noses are terrible."

"Theirs are. Their pets aren't."

"Pets?"

"Just stay close. Hopefully, I can skip the explanation."

Don't count on it.

I wasn't going to force the issue while in human territory, however. We stayed within the trees until the lines ended. Ahead, the plants were more like vines and leaves that lay on the ground. They didn't have much of a scent either. In the distance, I could see a cluster of the human boulders, and I think a rock beast or two. All of them still, silent, and dark. According to Luna, all good things.

Tilhack looked around, testing the air again, as well as perking his ears in every direction. He definitely knew more than he was saying.

"This way. We should be clear so long as—"

His ears shot up toward the human boulders at deep barking. First one set, then another. While not quite the sounds I was used to, the message was the same. "Get out! This is my territory"

Parts of the human boulders lit up. Tilhack gasped. I tensed for a fight.

"Wolfor protect us," Tilhack said. "Run for it, Wolf!"

He tore across the field, and I struggled to match his pace. His legs moved faster than I'd ever seen, yet his head kept searching back and forth for something. Perhaps for humans, I don't know. I was too busy burning my legs to keep up. Panting became a fight for air. Territory was swallowed whole in breaths past ordered fields of plants I'd never seen before. The barking chased after us, though it was getting quieter, so at least the dogs weren't catching up to us.

Tilhack changed his sprint to follow a well worn path between the fields. I could see more of the spider thread ahead of us, as well as some kind of flat branches that filled in one section of the barrier. It was as if someone had flattened some short trees, and attached them to trees between the spider thread barrier.

Tilhack went right toward the branches. I couldn't catch enough breath to ask why. Stopping didn't seem like a good idea either. That is until he slipped right under the branches as if they weren't there. I slid to a stop trying to figure out how he'd managed it.

"Right here, Wolf," he said. "Flatten yourself, work your front paws forward. Let them pull you along under the branches. Use your nose to guide you through the ditch in the ground. Keep your ears flat."

That sounded so much easier than it looked. His "ditch" wasn't much more than a dip in the dirt. The barking started getting louder. I saw two figures come tearing along the fields after us. I thrust my nose for the "ditch", trying to put Tilhack's words to use. Took me a couple of thrusts before I got myself moving forward. I moved my front paws forward, trying to go as flat as I could muster.

"That's it, Estrella. Keep moving. Claw by claw. Don't go backwards."

I think I lost fur along the way, but after some wiggling, I found myself on the other side. A loud crash sent me whirling around expecting to see a thunderstorm. Instead, I saw two black colored dogs with little fur, and knobs where they'd lost their tails, pounding on the branches. They were still barking fury at us, but they couldn't, or wouldn't, slip under just as we had. They were also big, and their somewhat pointed heads made me glad we weren't testing ourselves against them.

Tilhack edged me on, and I wasn't going to argue. We continued at a sprint into the grass lands, until we hadn't heard the barks for some time. There I insisted we rest before my legs melted. Once we found a tree to provide shade, I more fell onto my side than lay down. I panted harder than I ever had before. Felt like I'd be panting all through to the morning.

Tilhack didn't flop like I did, but he also didn't waste any time putting his head on the ground. He was panting harder than I was. Not surprised given his speed in there.

When we'd both caught our breath a bit, Tilhack pulled himself upright, though he only raised his head. He looked where we'd just come from before coming back to me.

"*Those* were pets," he said. "Humans out here often have them to protect their territory. We're lucky that's all we faced."

I couldn't muster the will to sit up. I just looked at him, still panting on my side. "And again I must ask, how do you know so much?"

He turned his ears back, then started twitching again. "It's nothing you need to worry about. It's a private matter I'd rather not discuss."

Now I did heave myself up. I needed to show some kind of strength, even a tired one. "Tilhack, if I'm going to take you into my pack, I need to know I can trust you. How can I when you won't be honest with me?"

His ears fell. Looked about ready to cower. "You don't understand. No wolf does."

"You're right I don't. We're all wolves, yet you say that as if you aren't a wolf yourself."

"I'm not."

My ears shot up. I tilted my head, trying to understand what he could possibly mean. *Not a wolf? You look like one to me.* Okay, maybe his scent wasn't prefect, and his pelt wasn't normal, but beyond the bright blue eyes, these were not things to discount him.

Tilhack dropped his head. His ears were back in pain I didn't understand. I perked mine forward in patient attention, while also making it clear I wasn't going anywhere.

"My mother was a wolf," he said after a heavy sigh. "She taught me everything I know about hunting, packs, and Wolfor. But like me, she'd grown up in the city. There are a lot of wild dogs there. Dogs that escaped from humans. My father was one of them. He'd spent a few years living with humans until one day, they left their den, and never came back. He waited for days until he ran out of food and water. He managed to escape before he starved. My mother found him. She helped him learn to make it on his own. They mated, and I was one of their pups. I learned the wild from my mother. I learned of humans from my father. She always said I had his eyes. From what I understand, I have his pelt too. Or, half of it anyway."

I tried to ease him on while within, I tried to process what I was hearing. "I don't understand. If you're not a wolf, what are you?"

"A mix breed. Half wolf, half husky. A mutt trapped between worlds. Humans fear me for my wolf side. Wolves rejected me for the husky side. My brothers were killed by Hitlark. He sees half-breeds like me as vermin that need to be killed to protect the pureness of the wolf. He'd kill me too if he could. Some humans have tried to do the same. I can't go to either of them, which leaves me nowhere."

I might have laughed if he weren't in so much pain. As it was, I couldn't help being amused by the irony. *Another lone wolf.* It must be a curse of some kind. I keep finding these strange wolves with painful backgrounds. A pup killer, a pack defender that lost his own afterward, now a half-breed. What next? A wolf rejected by Wolfor himself?

"Something about this amuse you?" Tilhack said. I must have lost my control for a moment.

"Not at all," I said. "Just thinking about the wolves I've met recently. Luna, Carlin, now you? Is there anyone in this world that isn't ashamed of who they are?"

He glared at me, more than a little offended. "I have reason to be. I'm not natural. I shouldn't have been born. Wolves and dogs aren't supposed to mix."

"So what? Luna was banished because they thought he killed his brother. That didn't stop me from chasing after him."

"But would you chase me?"

That caught me off guard. At first, I couldn't figure out where that came from. As my mind settled, I still couldn't quite figure it out.

"What?" I said. "What do you mean?"

He looked out toward the East. He suddenly looked as timeless as Carlin. "All my life, I've wanted to be wanted. By a pack, a human,... a mate. No one ever has. Too much wolf or too much husky. Even the wild dogs don't want anything to do with me. I've wanted the wild because no one knows about dogs there. They wouldn't know what I am. They'd see the wolf, and accept him."

"Haven't I done that?"

"Not the way I'd like. Estrella, I know it's not possible, but I still want you. You're like nothing I've ever seen. Behind your fur is a wolf I'd give anything to be with. The perfect mate to fill what I've been missing. A mate already claimed by another."

Now I understand. The truth kept me calm, at least with him. This wasn't Darok trying to make me forget Luna. This was Tilhack wishing for something he knew couldn't be. How could I fault him for that? If anything, I was flattered. Some females go their whole lives never having a male show interest in them. In the last few days I'd had two express deep desires for me. One tried to force it. The other laid near me, wishing he could ask, even though he knew about Luna.

It hurt actually. Husky blood or not, he'd proven himself to be a wolf of good standing. Strong enough to share himself, yet wise enough to know the real situation. Were it not for Luna, I'd probably be getting far more intimate with him by now.

Like you almost did with Darok? The question burned within. Shamed me like nothing I'd ever felt. Despite my words, for a moment, I had again considered the idea of running with another. Tilhack at least was worthy, but that didn't absolve me. After so much effort, how could I, even for a moment, abandon Luna? He was still out there... I hoped. I owed it to him to continue my chase. Yet here I was, once again coming close to giving it... given *him,* up. How would he take it if he knew? What would it do to him?

My own ears fell in a brief cringe. Even though Luna didn't know, I felt the pain even so. My mind wandered to wherever he was. Would he take me back if he knew? How deeply would it wound him? What if he wasn't alive after all? What did I deserve then?

Tilhack's head flopped on his paws like he'd just missed his last meal of the moon. His sigh snapped me out of my mental hunt. I couldn't let it stand. He didn't deserve to sulk in that much pain. I may still be a part of Luna, but I could perk up my pack mate without damaging that. Besides, I'm not sure I had any intention of letting Luna know what I'd done. It would spare him the pain... and maybe spare me the same.

I found the strength to rise, though my legs weren't too happy about moving. I tapped my nose against Tilhack's cheek in a show of affection. He didn't react. I persisted until his head rose to meet me.

I looked him straight in the eye to be sure he would hear me.

"I would chase you. Had I never met Luna, you'd be a fine wolf, and I do mean, *wolf.* Your blood is my blood. Your fangs are as sharp as mine. Your ears as keen. Your howl as strong. You are a wolf. You will always be a wolf, no matter what other blood runs through your veins."

Tilhack turned away, but not out of shame. His ears were too high for that. He took another look at the horizon. His ears turned forward with an amused huff. He came back to me with a glow back in his face.

His reply never got out. His ears shot up, facing past me. I turned mine the same direction, expecting to hear our bird singing some ridiculous song again. Instead, I heard a pair of barks joined with the barks of humans coming up behind us. The humans I hadn't heard before. The dogs were far too recent to forget.

"You can't be serious," I said. "How did they find us?"

"Like I said, some pets have some pretty good noses."

I looked back the way we'd come, but couldn't see them. The barks were quiet, suggesting we had a chance.

"They sound far away." I turned back to Tilhack as he shook himself to his paws. "I say we run for it. Humans don't have our endurance."

"Not sure we do either right now."

"Have a little faith. We'll outlast them. We're wolves, remember?"

He snorted with a forward tick of his ears. Then he turned and ran, with me right behind him.

My legs were not happy to say the least, but the threat of the humans had loosened them up. We didn't push ourselves as hard this time since we knew the humans were far slower than we were. Still wasn't long before our tongues were flapping in the air with each step. I tried to ignore the growing pain and heavieness in my legs. I couldn't ignore the sting in my side. Nor could I allow either to slow me down.

Tilhack angled for a patch of tall trees closer to those of my home. They still looked ordered somehow, but with no other sign of humans, we decided to risk it. We charged ahead, hopeful the terrain would slow the humans, who naturally wouldn't let their pets go too far ahead of them. Tilhack rounded a tree just ahead of me.

Then he vanished.

Something grabbed him so fast, I didn't realize he was gone until I'd run past where he'd been. His yip stopped me more than his disappearance did. When I turned to look, I found him tangled in a tightly woven spider web that hung him just above me. He was grunting and turning, trying to stand inside, only to slid around on his back again.

My nose searched for blood, or for the spider that had made the web. "You all right?"

"I can't get out," he said. "Can't get through this webbing either." We both looked toward the barks as they reached our ears again. While they were still a fair distance away, it wouldn't be long until they caught up with us. "Estrella. Save yourself. Get out of here while you can."

Now I know how Luna felt. I'll never forgive myself for it either. I couldn't bear the thought of running away from a pack mate when he needed me most. Worse, I couldn't live with myself knowing I'd forced him to die alone. No wolf should have to face that. I couldn't leave him there. Nor could I shake the fear that perhaps Luna wasn't alive after all.

"Over my dead body," I said to both Luna's and Tilhack's deaths. "I'm getting you out of there."

Tilhack growled, though at me or at being unable to stand I couldn't say. "You can't! You don't have time to do anything."

"Not if you keep arguing I don't. Now quit talking and start chewing. Don't make me force the issue like I did with my stupid den-mate."

He allowed a moment to consider before getting his teeth on whatever webbing he could. I reared up on my hind legs, put my paws on him, and started biting at the same spot.

The webbing was tough. Felt more like tight strands of hair or hard plant than webbing. Unlike the rock that caught me however, this trap was yielding. Strand by strand, we worked to free him. As the barks got louder, I worked harder. Tilhack tried to protest, but I snarled at him before he could say a word.

Strands broke one by one. We bit, tore, pulled with all we had. Eventually, part of the webbing gained some slack to it. I pulled hard on it, forcing me down on my paws again. Several strands broke with the one. Tilhack tumbled out of the webbing with a thump and another yip.

He didn't get to stand before it became a yelp of pain. The dogs charged right into us. The first bit into Tilhack's shoulder, while the other leapt at me, jaws open wide. I saw him just in time to avoid anything more than a small cut on my flank.

I heard the snarls and yelps of Tilhack's struggle, but I couldn't worry about him. I had a snarl of my own as the second dog was going after me again. He half barked half snarled as he attacked. He used his paws a lot too, reaching for my underside and legs. I used my own to keep his jaws away from my neck. His still bit my legs, my shoulder, a glancing blow on the side of my neck. A better bite took a chunk of flesh off my leg.

I did more damage though. My fur provided some protection, while he had none to speak of. His fur was so thin, every bite and claw strike drew blood. Solid bites drew a lot of blood. In seconds, his right foreleg was more red than black. Didn't stop him though. He still bit and snarled, trying to do whatever damage he could, and he was doing his fair share.

I managed to pull away from him after knocking him down. He rolled on the ground before charging at me. The damage to his leg and the blood loss had taken their toll. He couldn't hide a limp in his bloodied leg, nor the deep breaths he needed to breath at all. He snapped at my muzzle. I snapped his good foreleg in half. He fell to the ground, rolling as if trying to find his footing. I didn't let him. I pushed past his ruined legs. His jaws only slowed me down. I snapped at his neck, landing bite after bite until one found his windpipe. He gasped a moment, allowing me to bite and hold until he'd stopped moving once and for all.

I looked for Tilhack, snarling at whoever was there. I found the other dog already dead, covered in blood. Tilhack had moved on to a human he had on his back. Blood flowed from wounds on Tilhack's side. Must have been why the human was able to keep

Tilhack's jaws away from him with his paws. A second human was just turning my way, a thunder stick in his paws.

I didn't wait. I lunged right into the second human before he could do anything. He stumbled backward, falling over Tilhack and his companion. Tilhack was forced to retreat, but the human had lost hold of his thunder stick. Both humans crawled along the ground away from me as I stepped over their thunder stick. I showed them every bloody fang I had. Every hair stood on end. My snarl shook every bone in my body. I dared them to continue the fight.

They refused the challenge. They tripped over each other several times in a sprint away from us. I snarled after them until I felt sure they weren't coming back. In my state, I wasn't going to risk a longer fight. I could feel my fur wet with my own blood. My left fore-leg wasn't happy about missing part of it, though so long as it stayed uninfected, it wouldn't slow me down for long.

I turned to check on Tilhack, only to find him on his side, panting hard. Each breath was a struggle, and no wonder. His legs and chest were full of blood, most of it his. The ground under him suggested he was losing more by the minute.

And I could do nothing.

I laid beside him rubbing my head against his. He returned the rub even as he continued to fight for breath.

"Wouldn't change a thing," he said.

I gave him a snarl of my own.

"Don't you dare talk like that. You'll be fine. We're safe now."

"Too much... Fading fast... No chance."

"There is always a chance! Have a little faith. Wolfor didn't bring us together just so I could lose you now. My pack needs you, Tilhack. I need to find you a mate. I can't do that if you—"

I flinched when something sharp pricked my shoulder. I expected to find a bee or wasp. Found some kind of odd feather instead. I ignored it and continued to rub against Tilhack.

I gave him as much support as I could, even as I started to fade myself. My wounds weren't serious, yet I felt more and more tired by the second. Soon, my vision blurred, and I could barely move. It got so bad that I couldn't keep myself up at all. My head hit the ground, and I couldn't find the strength to lift it back up. I heard something, but my mind was too foggy to understand what it was. I thought I felt human paws just before everything faded.

Chapter 4

First thing I noticed was a headache the size of a full grown moose. Only thing that helped was how tired I felt as I slowly re-awoke to the world. Between the pain and the fog, I almost wanted to curl up and go back to sleep. My mind started clearing when I forced myself to stand. That was when I first noticed Tilhack wasn't there.

I looked around, and found I wasn't where I had been either. I was trapped in another of the humans' rocks, though this one had more of that stiff spider thread blocking one side. The sides of the rocks held slits half way down I could see through, but the rock was still too strong for me to break through. I pawed at the webbing, and found that it wasn't going to budge either.

I took deep breaths to keep myself calm while looking outside in an effort to find Tilhack. I found more humans instead. They were all walking around, barking and grumbling at each other, with no attention given to me at all. Behind them, I saw more of their temporary dens, though these were much larger than what Luna had described. The humans held all kinds of rocks and slabs, some times holding them up to their ears while barking to no one at all.

Tilhack was nowhere to be found. I couldn't find his scent anywhere on the wind either. Assuming it wasn't masked by burnt meat, tangy-sweet, and something close to wood, yet somehow crisper than your normal tree sap. *Did they leave him there to die?*

A human appeared on the other side of the webbing. She squatted down and looked right at me. The corners of her mouth curved upward, not sure why, though I could sense a lighter attitude from her. Something in her scent suggested she was amused, entertained, or perhaps cheerful. Not emotions I cared to share with her.

After a moment, I rose my hackles and showed her my fangs when I recognized her. She was the same human from before. The same pup that was arguing with the humans that carried me away from Luna. My growl rumbled within, daring her to try something.

Another human pulled her away. He looked like the older one she had been fighting with before. Probably her father, alpha, or both. He didn't have kind barks for her, not that she ever surrendered to them. I fell silent, but didn't stop watching them, until both were called inside one of the dens.

With little else to do, I turned to tend to my wounds. Except I found someone already had. My fur was clean. Cleaner than I'd ever gotten it, though some parts had been removed down to my skin. My cuts had already begun to heal enough that biting at an itch beside them didn't open them up again.

Vague memories returned. Foggy images of me on my side, my paws wrapped together, and my muzzle held shut by something. There were humans too. Several of them had been rubbing me, poking me with things I couldn't see, and working with my fur. *Were they... were they caring for me?* Luna would scoff at the idea, and frankly, so did I. After being taken away from my home, attacked by them and their pets, hunted by them in the forest, I couldn't believe any human would care for me like that.

The father and pup returned, this time carrying another rock like mine. A faint hope perked my ears toward it. *Do they have Tilhack in there?* Half of me prayed he was, though the other half wondered if he were better off dead. They set the rock next to mine, and the father nearly dragged his pup away despite great protest.

I looked out through the slits, trying to catch a scent. The humans' many scents clouded what little smell of wolf I did find. I couldn't be sure.

"Tilhack?" I said. "Tilhack, are you in there?"

A groaning whine was my first reply. Sounded like him... I think. Then his eyes appeared through one of the slits in his rock. Those were unmistakable.

"Estrella? That you?"

I would have bounded if I weren't confined. "It's me. You all right?"

Another groan. I heard him shake himself. "I feel like I haven't slept for days. I hurt like I just fought off a pair of mastiffs."

"You did, though I don't know if what you fought were mastiffs. Did fight a human though."

"Oh yeah. Now I remember. What... Where are we? What's with all the humans?"

"You don't know?"

"Not this time. Although I think... I think they healed me. My wounds aren't as bad as they were."

"Impossible. No human would bother..."

The female pup returned, this time with scraps of meat in her paws. I have to admit, my mouth watered when I saw them. I don't think I'd had much to eat while the humans had been doing... whatever it was they were doing to me. The pup made a ruffling sound much like a prey animal. I turned my head trying to understand it, to which she made the sound again.

She looked back at her father, then squatted down in front of me. My ears fell, and I retreated back into my rock, though I never quite managed a growl. She made soft barks while she pushed a strip of meat through the spider thread. My nose tested it first. My ears rose to watch for any deception

She sat there, still as a stone, not making a sound. I eased forward, one paw at a time. I watched her while my nose guided me to the meat. It smelled all right, and she didn't seem to have any ill intentions toward me. I licked the meat once. Cold, but still meat. I snatched it in my jaws, and retreated again before she could reclaim it. I swallowed it whole, grateful to have anything in my stomach.

We repeated this ritual several times, before she moved over and did the same with Tilhack. He was a little quicker to approach, but was no less wary of her. I never let her out of my sight, even after she left us.

"Well," Tilhack said. "looks like humans aren't all bad."

I glared at him, even though I couldn't see him. "Don't let food cloud your judgment. These humans are dangerous creatures. They've been hunting us for years. They almost killed us back there."

"And Hitlark is both irrational, and short tempered. There is good and bad in all beings Estrella. Perhaps we've only seen the bad ones."

Aren't they enough? It was the "bad ones" that injured Luna, captured me, killed entire packs. And for what? Luna said they rarely took anything besides our skins. Perhaps these weren't going to do the same, but that did nothing to change what they were, or how I felt about them.

"Reason enough to avoid all," I said. "We do just fine without them. It's when they try to kill us they become a problem."

I heard Tilhack growl. Without being able to see him, I couldn't say why. "I'd like to disagree, but after those two humans and their dogs, it's hard to. Guess I still have a bit to learn about being a wild wolf."

If only I could give him a tap to ease his nerves. "You'll be fine. Just stay alert. They'll make their mistake. When they do, we..."

I stopped when I saw a few humans approaching a pair of new arrivals. The father and daughter followed as well. I tried to see, but they went past my field of view.

I could hear their barks though. Loud, energetic, and some sounded quite angry. Stress filled the air like a thick fog. I could smell it and feel it all around me. Something important was happening. Something I didn't want to be around for. I knew I couldn't escape, which left me to feel the tension pick at me like fangs from a mouth I couldn't see. I wanted to run, but I couldn't even hide. I could only check every peep hole, frantic to find a way out, or at least to see what was going on.

The father and pup returned with the new humans. I growled at them, as did Tilhack, the moment we got a good look at them. *I should have recognized their scent.* They were the same humans who had just attacked us. One showed his foreleg to the father. Tilhack had left a pretty nasty wound behind. *Not bad for a city wolf.*

The father looked at us, then shook his head with a sigh. A gesture I didn't understand since it was too slow to achieve anything, yet it seemed to make the pup go crazy. She tugged and barked at her father as if she were in pain. When the father pushed her away, my ears fell as I felt the tension reach new heights. *This can't be good.* Instinct saw my hackles raise, and my growl grow into a snarl. I had no other choice. Without the ability to run, hide, or fight, I could only warn them of the danger they held captive.

The father shook his head again. The pup breathed like she might heave her heart out. She screamed so loud it almost hurt, but the father ignored her. On his command, one of the other humans held her while he went into one of the dens.

He returned with a thunder stick.

My snarl grew, and my focus fell squarely on him. I grew tight despite my display. I couldn't run, couldn't fight, couldn't do anything but threaten. I felt certain this time, they really were going to kill me, and I had no way to stop it. I tried to warn him off in the only hope I had. He ignored it as he stood in front of me. Tilhack echoed my snarl, actually reached a point where it was louder than mine. All it did was make the human pause a moment.

I heard screaming and more barking from the pup. The father continued to ignore her. So did I. She meant nothing to me at the moment. That is until without warning, she stood right in front of me. My growl vanished as I was startled by her approach. *Must have missed her breaking free of the other human's hold.* The father snarled fury at her, and she snarled right back. They barked at each other for some time. The two new humans barked as well, until the father shut them up with one, loud bark that even had my ears falling.

The father barked again, this time at his pack. The other humans started walking toward the pup like they were going to attack. The pup barked again, then turned around, and appeared to open the spider webbing. Before I had a chance to think, loud thumping on the top of my rock sent me sprinting away on reflex. I tore out of the rock right beside Tilhack doing the same.

The other humans went crazier than a spooked herd. Some barked in a frenzy, some ran away though they didn't appear afraid, some couldn't seem to decide what to do or where to go. Many of them tried to form a barrier to stop us. The two humans we fought before dove into one of the dens in a panic I could smell for miles. The father leveled his thunder stick.

Tilhack and I never stopped moving. We found a hole in their line, and we bolted for it. We slipped right past them, sprinting into what I only now realized was a very thin forest. Thunder never followed, but that didn't slow me down. If anything, it made me ignore everything that didn't lie in my current path.

We kept running. Tilhack and I ran at full speed away from the humans, worrying only about not running into things, and not losing each other. My legs burned. My sides weren't far behind. After a time I was too scraed to track, I saw Tilhack gasping for breath, and realized we couldn't go any further. We didn't bother to find a good spot this time. I stopped us amid trees closer to those of home, and Tilhack collapsed on his side, panting so hard I feared he might damage his lungs.

I laid beside him, panting only a little softer. I rubbed my head against his, to which he looked up with a perk in his ears.

"You're not... changing your mind about... Luna are you?"

I panted a chuckle at him, though I did turn my ears back as well. *Not this time.* "No. But I am glad you made it."

"I'll take that."

I ruffed amusement. *As well you should.* I nuzzled on his wounds, and found they too had sealed up while we were asleep.

"Your wounds still feel okay?" I asked.

He ticked his ears forward, though never lifted his head. "Still hurt though. No thanks to our escape."

"Well, we could always go back if you want."

He laughed, then forced himself to sit up. Took a few whines to do it. "I'll pass, thanks. Thanking that pup isn't worth the risk."

I almost pinned him for suggesting it. The idea got wounded by the pain in my sides. It died when I let myself really think about it.

What happened back there? Did those humans care for us? Heal us? What about that pup? I couldn't get any of what she did to make sense. All I knew of humans was thunder sticks and rock beasts. Things to be afraid of. The thought of being helped by one...

"I must be losing it," I said. "I mean, it's impossible. She didn't save us... did she?"

Tilhack looked at nothing for a moment. Long enough for me to worry. He returned to the present before I decided to check on him.

"I think she did," he said. "Can't imagine why. Not that I understand humans half as well as I sound. Do you think she had a reason? Some strange urge to do something for us?"

I turned my ears back, too tired to fight with it. "I suppose we'll never know. Still, I think we owe it to her to do something."

"Like what? You want to take a rabbit to her or something?"

I was my turn to laugh again. *Somehow, I don't think she'd appreciate it like we would.*

"No. But we should pray for her."

Tilhack's ears perked and his head tilted confusion. "To who? The wolves of the after life?"

"No. To Wolfor himself."

Chapter 5

The bird found us soon after our escape. He didn't stop singing, though his songs gave me so much joy. Home was close. So close the scents were turning familiar. The trees, the prey, the air, this is where my heart belonged. Now I just had to find the other half.

At one point, the bird flew ahead of us. I didn't ask why, because we'd just crossed one of Luna's markings. He no doubt had gone in search of Luna. Even if he hadn't, it gave me a chance to actually say something I'd been considering since Tilhack told me what he was.

It hurt though. It meant keeping something from Luna. It was for his own good, or so I told myself. Truth is, I didn't want to face it either. I wanted to forget it all. I wanted to leave it all behind as we had the last pack of humans. I couldn't of course. It would always be there. A small scar I'd have to live with.

That did not mean Luna had to share it.

"Tilhack," I said. "Don't tell Luna about Darok. Don't let him know that I… that I almost replaced him. Or that I killed another wolf for no real reason."

Tilhack stopped while he turned his head in confusion. "What? You never said anything about that."

I didn't? But surely I... no. I only told him he had forced himself on me. I never told him the rest.

"Darok did force himself on me, but I… I had begun to accept my captive life. Enough that I'd considered taking him as my mate. I've been through so much to be with Luna, the thought that, even for a moment, I might replace him... Tilhack, I can't do that to him. He's been hurt far more than you can imagine. Please, don't tell him. Don't ever tell him that I ever pursued another wolf."

"Where does that leave me?"

The question hurt as much as the memory. Yes, I had briefly pursued him too. After our escape, we'd shared some moments of affection. Moments that I rather enjoyed. They couldn't compare to Luna, but they were there all the same. I could feel his desire then. He never pushed. He'd even appeared to accept that I wasn't available. Still, the affection showed him how much I cared. It shamed me, more so now that we were so close to finding my true mate.

"I suppose that's up to you," I said. "Luna is my mate, but I still want you with us. Our pack needs more members. Mix-breed or not, you are a wolf I want in my pack. But if you don't feel comfortable, I won't make you stay. I can't say what else you'll find however."

Tilhack's ears shifted in thought, but only briefly. "I would run with you, Estrella. I know you have a mate, I've accepted that. But just as you want me, I still want to be near you. I can think of no other place I could go. Even if there were, I can't see myself going there. If Luna will have me, I will join your pack."

I offered a deep rub of affection along his muzzle. He returned it without a word. We didn't need any. He was fine with his situation, and so was I. I didn't even need to ask again about Darok. For Luna's sake... and for mine, we wouldn't speak of it. Not unless we felt we had to. As for Luna accepting him, I wouldn't tolerate him not.

We continued our journey into Luna's territory. I kept my ears up and nose testing with every step. Then the bird reappeared overhead, gliding over us.

"Follow quickly soon ahead, Luna Luna far from dead!"

He flew past us, but in a straight line. An easy path to follow. Tilhack stayed close as I ran toward my other half. I could feel him even though I couldn't see him. Perhaps just my emotions, but I didn't care why. I just wanted to get his fur against mine.

The bird's chirping suggested we'd find Luna just ahead. And so we did, somehow in just the place I would have expected.

The mostly black colored Rajor was there with his pack, looking at

Luna… rather oddly actually. It was enough to stop me nearby. This wasn't the same mocking brother I'd seen before. He was different. He was carrying himself as if… as if proud of something other than himself. His pups maybe? I could see them near by, with Lonate of course. *Dose that wolf go anywhere without pups near him?*

I also wondered if I should wait before I let Luna find me. Perhaps in the middle of a duel with Rajor wasn't the best time to learn your dead mate isn't dead. Then again, it might be exactly the perfect time, especially if a fight broke out. As such, I decided to watch and wait to see which choice felt most right.

With the wind coming at us, Luna hadn't found me, and thus only had attention for his bird.

"What are you doing back?" he said. "I thought I'd chased you off for good."

We could only be so lucky.

The bird chirped joy. "Like the sun and rain, I shall remain, flying near you, help your pain."

"I don't know about that, but I can't say I'm not glad to see you. Where have you been anyway."

"Searching searching I did go, found found yours plus more."

Rajor stared at the bird more perplexed than anything else. "Yours plus more? What in Wolfor's name are you talking about?"

Now was the time. It would stick in Rajor's jaw, and it would be a joyous shock for Luna. Yes, it was the perfect time to announce myself.

I stepped forward, drawing myself up with pride. *Time to come home.*

"He means me, Rajor."

Luna's head snapped my way so fast it's a wonder he didn't break his own neck. Once his eyes found me, he seemed to freeze in a premanant perked position. *Perfection.* However, when he stayed that way for a long moment, I realized he needed an extra nudge to get him moving.

So I gave him one.

"Aren't you going to say anything, Thorn?"

His sprint toward me made it all worth it.

Tainted Blood

Prologue

As alpha, the lead wolf must care for the pack. Their health, their well being, their very survival, rests with him or her or those that lead. It is why only a few can carry the weight. Why only those with the blood can fulfill the role. Even then, there are times when the best of alphas, can make the gravest of errors.

Chapter 1

I could hear her snarls despite the great distance. No one knew of course. The rest of the pack were back at the meeting area, caring for the pups. As for me... call it instinct, my heart, or Wolfor's guidance, but when I saw Barkera tear into the forest, I followed.

What is wrong with her? She'd been acting strange lately. Her once eternal temper had vanished in favor of aggression that lashed out for no particular reason. Members were being snarled and snapped at for things they weren't even doing. That was when she wasn't attacking... well... anything. Branches, shadows, even prey. She seemed to be trying to kill anything she could get her teeth into because she was mad at it. This was not the alpha wolf I knew. This was not the mother that had raised me. Something was wrong, and I was determined to find out what.

Or rather, I was determined to show myself something *else* was wrong. My father, Dunil, had told me about the rage plague. A disease that sometimes affects wolves and other animals. It always led to immense aggression, and eventually, a painful death. Barkera had shown signs of it despite my prayers to the contrary. I had tried to mention it to Dunil, but he had brushed me off. "She's just old," he'd said. Try as I might, I didn't think so. I thought... I feared, Barkera had the rage plague. If I was right, she was a danger to the pack and... must be dealt with.

Thus, I followed her that night. She'd gone deep into the forest, past the edges of our territory. I kept to the shadows, staying hidden while keeping her in sight. My pelt of mostly dark grey, with brown touching my back, tail, and ears, proved useful in staying out of sight. The winds blew my scent back at me to keep me hidden from her nose.

Barkera came into view as she stopped to search the air for something. Her fur, a dark brown that was nearly black with lighter brown highlights, looked very much like tree bark. I was told that she'd shown a similar protectiveness as a pup, as if she covered herself in a layer of bark to keep herself safe. Thus was the origin of her name. Fortune, or perhaps Wolfor's influence, saw her fur grow to match it.

She continued to sniff at the air, looking around and growling at nothing as she did. Every hair stood on end, her ears were frozen in full display, even her tail seemed to snap at times like an agitated cougar. It was as if she were in the middle of a rival pack, yet she stood alone, save for me in the shadows just ahead of her, trying to stay with the changing winds. Our solitude may have been a blessing, for she had nothing to attack that would be a threat.

That is until lights showed in the distance to my side. It was an odd glow I had seen too many times before. *Great, more humans.* They'd been making more appearances lately, always carrying some kind of rocks that either had pebbles that glowed like the sun, or the rocks themselves cast strong beams of light in one direction. Were it not for the mockingbirds, I wouldn't know what they were called, much less the danger they posed. Thankfully, most of them had given our pack a wide berth, though their thunder-sticks could still be heard in the distance on occasion.

Barkera looked toward this glow, and instantly snarled as if she were about to tear it apart. With the snarl came frothing of the mouth, a crazed look in her eyes, and a sink of my stomach. There it was. The final confirmation. She had the rage plague. My own mother was doomed to a painful death, assuming something else didn't kill her.

I turned to leave, only to catch Barkera sprint toward the light. My heart joined my stomach at the bottom of my paws. *No. No, don't go after the humans. Please no.* But she was, and in an instant, I was after her. I don't know where the decision had come from, only that

I'd made it. Thank Wolfor I'd been ahead of her, or I'd have never caught her.

"Barkera!" I called, hoping it might stop her. "Barkera stop. You can't—"

It stopped her all right.

"You dare talk to me like that, Carlin?! I'll see you put in your place for good!"

She turned straight around and turned her jaws toward me. She didn't say another word. She just snarled death as she charged toward me.

A sane Barkera would have torn me apart with ease, but she was far from sane. Even as she ran, there was just the smallest touch of unbalance to her, as if her legs sometimes landed in places she didn't mean to put them. This was my only chance. I braced myself, not bothering to snarl. It would do no good.

Barkera continued her charge. She leapt the final stretch as if she might leap right through me. That gave me the opening I needed. I dove under her and caught her throat in my jaws. She landed with a thump, and I bit down as hard as I could. Barkera snapped, snarled, and clawed, even as she hacked through her crushed windpipe. Her claws raked across my muzzle, leaving deep cuts just in front of my left eye. I held my grip, trying to ignore the thorn in my heart, or the struggle to breathe through it, as I ended her life. Finally, her struggles slowed, slowed, and at last, she fell limp in my jaws. I held a moment longer to be sure before letting her go.

For a long time, I could only stare at her. My own mother. I knew I had to, she had left me no choice. Going after anything that moved is one thing. Going after humans... she'd become a danger to the pack. She... *I'd had no choice.* That didn't change the fact that she was dead. That *I* had killed her. Loss is loss. Being responsible for that loss, no matter the reason... *I'd had no choice.*

I let my heart ache while I tried my best to care for my wounds. Being on my muzzle, there wasn't much I could do. That and there was this little problem of me possibly contracting the rage plague myself. Barkera's neck was oddly lacking in terms of blood despite my bite. Truth be told, I couldn't be sure how much of the blood in my mouth was from my own wound. Would I join her in her fate? Would Dunil do to me what I'd done to her?

Maybe not. No one really knew how one got the rage plague. Maybe I'd be fine. Maybe I'd escape it. I prayed, I begged Wolfor to give me that much. The fear didn't go away. Neither did the pain every time I looked at my mother's body. The loving, caring, crazy mother I once knew, the immovable rock of the pack, now gone. My fault or not, that loss would hurt for a long, long time.

Fear and pain kept me from feeling anything as I made my way home. I could barely think of what to do with myself, to say nothing of... *oh Wolfor's fang, Dunil. What am I going to say to him?!* I'd just killed his mate. Considering the fact that he'd rejected the possibility of the rage plague... *I'd had no choice. Oh, that'll go over well.*

I found myself at the stream near the pack's meeting area. It was barely ankle deep and about as wide, but it was a source of cool water. The pups loved playing in it too. From the sounds breaking through my mental fog, it would appear that's what they were doing.

Then the fog cleared, and my heart and stomach found a new low.

The pups were playing all right, except for two of them. They were sitting at the edge, glaring and growling their puppy growl at anyone who passed by. This alone meant little, until one of their siblings splashed them.

Both pups recoiled as if a tree had fallen right in front of them.

"Hey!" one said. "Watch it you stupid whelp! I don't want that getting on me!"

Dunil moved in to reprimand, but I was busy watching the two pups. Pups I'd seen Barkera bite sharp enough to draw blood a few days ago. *No. Please Wolfor no. Don't... don't let it be.* Yet the more I watched, the more it was there. The aggression, the jitters, and that one eternal symptom; fear of water. Dunil didn't seem to notice. He went on trying to discipline, but the pups were only snarling back at him. Not much of a snarl at their age, but... but...

I cringed so hard I felt I might collapse into myself. I knew what I had to do. Dunil clearly wasn't going to. If he couldn't see Barkera's illness, there's no way he'd see his own pups in the same condition. I also knew what it would cost me.

But Barkera… she'd told me from a young age, the pack comes first. If these pups weren't… dealt with, they would threaten the pack. Once again, I had no choice. Siblings or not, I had to protect my pack. Regardless of the consequences.

I left my heart behind as I rushed for the pups. Dunil was snarling death in their face, and they were trying to snarl the same back. He yelled at them and they ignored it. Dunil snapped at one of their muzzles. One pup tried to do the same.

His bite never landed. My jaws landed on his neck before he could make contact. Without hesitation, I bit down and snapped the pup's neck like a twig. While the pack watched in horror, I did the same to the second pup. Grab, bite, *snap,* and just like that, the threat to the pack was gone. *At least it better be. Wolfor so help me, if more are infected I'll—*

"Carlin! What have you done?!"

Dunil's voice echoed off the trees. I cringed pain as I knew what was coming next. What I was about to do to my father.

"They had the rage plague, Dunil," I said. "So did Barkera. I had no—"

"Barkera? Where is she? Where is she?!"

Tell me this gets easier. "She's dead. I had to kill her too. She was about to—"

Dunil had me on the ground before I knew what happened. He snarled fury while biting into my neck. He clamped down so hard I couldn't get the breath to whine. *Well, I guess I knew this was coming.* I tried to surrender, even though I knew death was coming.

Except it didn't. Husita, a young, black-furred female we had taken in, managed to bite enough to get Dunil to release his hold. Well, more accurately, he released his hold so he could pin her, but she'd given me the chance to breathe. While Husita surrendered enough for Dunil to let her go, I rolled onto my paws and did the same.

Dunil looked back to me with all the rage he'd just shown. "You expect that to be enough? After you killed my mate, *your mother,* and *two* of my pups?"

I pinned my ears back as far as they would go. "I had no choice. They were a threat to the pack. I had to—"

"Get out. Leave my territory. I hereby declare you a lone wolf! You shall never know the joy of running with a pack again. You will live your life forever alone."

Husita rose and sent everyone's ears up by snarling her anger. "You can't do that! He did what he had to for the sake of the pack. If you weren't so blind you'd see—"

"Husita, stop!" My voice came out so fast I don't know when I'd decided to speak. But my words came all the same, and I knew they were right as they did. "I've killed an alpha female, my own mother no less, and two of her pups. I am as much a threat to the pack as they were. I will face my fate. Take care of the pack for me. Keep them strong."

Husita tried to speak, but all she could manage was a forward tick of her ears.

Dunil however, didn't wait long. "Get moving, murderer. Let me never find your scent again, or I will make sure it is the last time you leave it."

I ticked my ears forward in understanding. I then turned and ran. I kept running long after I'd passed my father's scent markings. When I finally stopped, I'd run so far I could barely hear the howl of mourning for the wolves lost.

I knew Husita was sneaking in a howl for me. She'd spoken highly of me, and had mentioned many times that she saw me as her example. It was kind of flattering really. *Good. Maybe today she'll see what a wolf must sometimes do for their pack.*

If I was honest, I knew I didn't deserve to be banished. Lone wolf? Didn't deserve that either. But Dunil, he'd always been impulsive. His emotions drove him more than his mind. Barkera had been the wise side of the pack. At least, until the rage plague took her. I could only imagine what the pack would be like without her. I didn't think it would suffer much. Dunil might be impulsive, but he led well. Once he stopped hurting, he'd be fine.

As for me, as I got honest with myself, I realized that the real reason I'd accepted my fate was I didn't want to become a risk. I'd killed Barkera, and then two pups, all with clear signs. The chances of me getting the rage plague were near certain. Best I get it out here, away from wolves and humans alike. When I finally went crazy, I'd do it alone.

Yes, I was a lone wolf, but given the circumstances, I was okay with that. After all, I wasn't going to be *any* wolf for very long.

Chapter 2

It's a good thing I'd decided to hunt as if I were going to live that day. At the time, I did it so I wouldn't suffer the pain of starving. I just didn't like the idea, though I had no idea how much pain the rage plague actually caused. Every day I waited for it to begin. Would I even recognize it? Or would I simply turn angry at everything, and fear water as if a single drop might kill me? I waited for it to come.

It never did.

Days passed. Then moons. Then a full year, and the only anger I felt was at the injustice of it all. I'd accepted my fate because I expected to become a risk. I was wrong, but now I'd have to endure a different fate. Wolves would be told of my "crime". No pack would take me. No loner would either. By saving my pack, I'd doomed myself to a lonely existence.

However, I *had* saved my pack. Every time I got close to brooding, that fact brought me back. Yes, I was wronged, banished when I didn't deserve it, but what choice did I have? Dunil couldn't, or wouldn't, see the truth. None of the others would act, not that I blame them really. It's hard to go against one's alpha. I'd made a choice to do what I had to for the sake of the pack. Knowing they were safe and able to thrive once more... lone wolf? I could live with that.

Or so I told myself.

A second year passed, and the pains of being alone grew every day. I'd wake under a tree, ready to join the hunt with my pack. Except there was no pack. Not for me. Then the excitement would turn to pain. I hadn't said a word to anyone since... since I'd killed my mother and brothers. I had no one to talk to. I could talk at the trees. I even tried it once. It only reminded me of my situation.

No wonder being made a lone wolf is the worst a wolf can suffer. My blood yearned for the company of another. Hunting wasn't as easy either. When the storms came, rains fell, and thunder clapped, I had only myself to curl against. When I was injured on a hunt, only I was there to care for the wound. I had no one to offer comfort in my fear. Instinct alone kept me going. I was alive, but I'm not sure I'd call it living.

So it was that on a summer morning, I was doing what I'd always done. Marked my small section of forest, checked some trails, and howled into the depths as much in pain as to announce my presence. I may be a loner, but even a lone wolf must claim one's borders. Besides, hearing the replies... well, it's better than hearing none at all.

Eventually, one trail led me to a freshly killed deer. A strong male, brought down by a cougar by the smell of it. Must not have been hungry, because there was a lot left. Beyond the risk of meeting said cougar, can't say I cared. Assuming the birds, or the original killer, didn't pick it clean too quickly, I'd have a food source for a few days. He'd even left me an untouched kidney. *Now there's a treat I haven't had in a while. Thank you, Wolfor.*

I dug into my find, enjoying every chunk of meat I swallowed more than I had in weeks. That is until I heard a rustling from nearby. My eyes and ears went up toward it. I worried the cougar had come back. I had so much blood on and in my muzzle, I couldn't be sure of the scents I could find, and the winds were blowing the wrong way as well. Unsure of the rival, my lips curled at another rustle to warn whatever it was that I intended to defend the kill. It didn't matter who had made it, it belonged to me now!

A familiar wolf of black fur emerged. White mixed heavily into her under-belly, chest, and face fur, though it never touched the top of her muzzle. I don't know if I never noticed before, or if it had changed, but it seemed like she had a fair bit of silver in her flanks and shoulders as well, reminding me a lot of a silver fox.

"Husita?" I said, dropping my display. "What are you doing out here? Is the pack with you."

Her ears flashed back, either in a cringe or submission, I'm not sure. "I left them a long time ago. I've been trying to find you."

My head tilted in confusion. "Why? Did Dunil revoke my sentence?"

She snorted at the very idea. "Hardly. In fact, he didn't live long after. A buck mauled him in a hunt. Came out of nowhere and stabbed his flank. Still got the kill, but his wounds... we did our best, but they got infected. All of them. He... I've never heard such cries. Yulina leads the pack now."

Now my ears fell in pure cringe. Try as I might not to, I imagined what it must have been like. Several wounds, all infected, the pain... it made my stomach turn just thinking about it. He'd wronged me, given me unfair punishment, but he didn't deserve that. No wolf did.

"I'm sorry," I said. "Though that doesn't answer my question. What are you doing out here?"

"I decided to chase the only wolf I know worth chasing. No one in the pack matches, and it's not like I have a chance of mating with Yulina, though even she wouldn't be a match even if I did. You were the one who convinced Dunil to take me in. You've been nothing but perfect since."

I don't know if I was truly confused, or my brain couldn't believe what it was hearing. I was flattered of course, even if her praises were a little misguided. I mean, perfect? I couldn't say I was anywhere close to that. Never mind the whole idea that she'd spent all that time looking for me. It warmed a part of my heart I'd forgotten was there. I don't know what I would have said under normal circumstances.

Considering my condition however, I had only one thing I *could* say. "Thank you, but it's not possible. I'm a lone wolf, remember? I am—"

"Oh, shut up. We both know you did what you did for the sake of the pack. Sometimes I wonder if Dunil didn't get exactly what he deserved because he couldn't accept the truth about Barkera. You don't deserve to live out here alone, and I refuse to let you or anyone else tell me otherwise. I don't care where I end up with you. I only care that I *remain* with you."

"I... uh... well the... but... you..." I'm not quite sure which emotion I felt. Flattered for sure. Embarrassed quite likely. Moved... not sure I want to say. "You... you do know how they'll react, right?"

My insides split into two wolves that warred with each other.

Really? That's the best you can come up with?

Oh, shut up.

Husita was equally unimpressed. "Would I be out here if I cared? I'm running with you, Carlin. And before you think it, good luck chasing me away. Now. What do you say to *that*?"

Can I have a few days?

"I... I think there's... still a kidney left."

Smooth. Very smooth.

Wolfor kill me now.

***

Ok, so having her to curl against me during a storm was nice.

Nice?! That's it?

I gotta stop arguing with myself.

Fine, it was amazing. It didn't matter that it was only her, it wasn't just me anymore. Feeling the warmth of another... I think I might have actually enjoyed that storm. True, it had something to do with the company, but that didn't make it feel any worse.

It didn't stop there. The two of us quickly became a perfect hunting pair. Rats and rabbits were easy kills. We were even finding success hunting the larger prey. Not perfect, as a serious gash on my leg proved. But even then, there she was, caring for my wound, keeping it from doing anything besides adding to my scars. Another wolf. Another soul resting with mine. I never realized how much I'd missed it.

Nor did I realize before how very wonderful she was.

I was flattered by her opinion of me. Okay, *very* flattered. At the time I didn't think much of it. It felt good, sure, but that's all it was. The warm feeling you get when someone gives you high praise. Nothing to fret over.

Of course as a reward, I had to offer her my affection in return. She'd come out searching for me, ignoring my sentence, determined to run with me. She deserved to have me nuzzle her any chance I got. To make sure I laid beside her every night. To ensure she got prime parts of a kill despite her technically being below me. And when I found a bird's egg that had fallen out of a nest in tact, why shouldn't I give it to her? I mean, she'd mentioned before how much she liked eggs, rare though her chances might be. It was the least I could do. The light in her eyes made it all worth it.

Again, nothing to fret over.

Uh-huh. Just keep on lying to yourself.

I thought I got rid of you.

I ignored the other side of myself while continuing my affection. She returned it often enough, though other times she seemed to ignore it. She never said anything. Just went on as if I hadn't done anything. That said, she never ignored my company. Any time we settled in to sleep, if I didn't go to her side, she would come to mine. Either way, she always made a point of pressing her body against me. In those moments, I swore I wouldn't breathe if it meant disturbing her.

Winter came and went. Our hunting ability kept us well fed despite a lack of game. Had we a full pack to care for, it might have been difficult. Then again, a full pack would have been able to go after herds we outright ignored.

Yet those thoughts never left me. From the first snow fall to the first blade of grass, the word "pack" kept echoing in my head. The two of us could barely be called such. Other loners might be taken in as she was, but would they want to? Even if they did…

"Carlin? What's wrong?"

She'd stirred from a nap under our favorite oak tree. I'd never fallen asleep. Rested yes, but sleep? My wind was too busy. It was this she saw, and this I had to address.

I feared the conversation, but knew it had to come.

"What are we doing?" I said. "I don't mean right now. I mean… what are we *going* to do? What is our future here?"

Her head tilted confusion. "What do you mean? Carlin, what's got you so worried?"

I wish I knew. "It's just… I… What are we doing? Are we fooling ourselves? Are we playing at something that will never be?"

"I haven't been playing at anything. I didn't think you were either. In fact, I thought we were doing quite well together. Or have I misunderstood your feelings towards me?"

OOoooo, the moment of truth. How does the young wolf respond?

By wishing you'd go away and never come back.

"You haven't," I said. "But, Husita... I..."

I'm scared.

I couldn't say it. I couldn't admit it. My ears fell as my insides hurt with the failed effort to force the words out. Why? Did I really think she'd leave me? She'd defied my punishment by searching for me. If that wasn't going to keep her away, how could my fear change anything?

Because your fear is yours. *Your punishment came from elsewhere.*

Oh, now you're on my side?

I always have been.

The source of my fear hurt almost as much as trying to admit it. What if I didn't measure up? What if I failed as alpha? What if I could never care for my pups properly?

What if I lost her?

Words never came. Just flattened ears and soft whines as I tried to force them out.

She silenced both by rubbing her head against mine. "I am too. Dunil had an established pack to rear his young. You and I have just each other. But, Carlin, you survived for two years alone. That means you can provide for our first litter without much more effort."

"But what of others? The pups of a lone wolf? What will others think?"

Really? You're going there?

It's a valid concern.

Bet it's not.

"Even if they know, what does it matter? They will be judged by their own merits. Packs will accept them or not for what *they* can do. Not for what their father did, which by the way, is quite a lot."

Now my ears fell in embarrassment. "All I did was kill my mother and two brothers."

"Who had the rage plague. You accepted your punishment because you thought you'd get it too. That says you put the pack first. How many wolves would go to such lengths for their pack."

"Any worth their fangs."

"I know a great many who would not be so quick. Don't forget, you killed your *alpha female.* Most wolves would never dream of attacking them, much less killing them, no matter what the reason. Most that would, would have fought Dunil over their punishment without any thought to the danger they themselves might become. Carlin, you are the best wolf I know. Your pups will be the same. I have no doubt of that."

Wow. Even I don't know what to say to that.

Glad we can agree on something.

My ears fell again. Pain, but the happy kind. Her support, her faith… it felt so good it hurt. I never would have dared hope to find a pack mate… a *mate,* of such character. Even now, as I laid there, trying to find words, she didn't pressure me. She stayed still, letting her fur mix with mine. She watched with respect for my reply, but nothing more.

Maybe I could do it. As she said, I'd kept myself well fed. The first litter would be the hardest, but I could do it. *We* could it. I know we could. I know we would.

"Thank you," I said. "I don't know what I did to deserve you."

"You killed your mother."

I recoiled in shock, only to play growl at her a moment later.

Another moment more and we were play fighting and laughing so hard we quickly ran out of breath. Two days later, she went into heat. Two moons later, she gave birth to six healthy pups. All but one survived their first year.

They would not be the last.

Chapter 3

Many years passed, most of them happy. There were the litters that only saw two pups survive. The year we lost three pack members to a lean winter. The year I spent two moons nursing a leg I was sure was broken, which was the same year I killed one of my pups when his pack and mine clashed over territory. I had added to my scars, though I learned well from each of them.

But as much as those years hurt, there were years of joy. Year after year of healthy litters. Seeing my pups grow, and learn, and become amazing wolves. The mixed emotions of them leaving to pursue, and often find, mates of their own. The loners we took in that made our pack that much better. The many days of hunting lessons, play fighting, days spent with my young while Husita hunted. It was so glorious, I was sure it wasn't happening to me. It was as if I were watching someone else live this perfect life.

Thus, I wasn't worried when fate saw us less than we had been. A harsh winter had claimed older loners. An ambush by a desperate cougar had claimed two more. The rest had dispersed to find packs and mates of their own. Thus, that year found us down to just me, Husita, two adults, and two "pups" from the previous litter. At least we had five healthy pups in our new litter. One that had been born far earlier than I'd ever seen. But Husita had gone into heat, and the game was good. Still, it made me nervous when there was still snow on the ground by the time the pups came out of the den.

Made me glad to have Lonate. He was the more impressive of the two older pups. Well, I suppose "pup" isn't accurate, as they were of adult age, even though they both still looked so young. Brezin was nearly solid black like his mother, with very little white to be found. Even then, it was mostly his underside and paws.

Lonate however, by Wolfor, he looked so much like me. His under side was mostly white, though black covered his back, neck, shoulders and top of his head, much like me. He barely had any brown at all though, and his face and throat were also white, making his stare rather impressive when he used it. Which he often did with his younger siblings. It allowed Husita and I to hunt together, leaving our next generation in the care of the previous. They were well cared for, and well watched.

Then one day, everything changed.

Most of the pack and I were coming come back from a hunt with the day's kill in our jaws. We arrived at the meeting area to find Lonate and Brezin frantically searching the area around the den. At first I thought they were trying to find some mouse or rabbit the pups could use to practice on.

That changed when Brezin spoke.

"I can't find him. I don't understand. How did Vinsi get away? And why can't I find his trail?"

The meal I had in my mouth fell to the ground. Vinsi? He was missing? I sprinted up to Lonate, who's ears fell when he saw me.

"Relax," I said. "You don't need to fear me. But what's going on?"

His ears never rose. "Vinsi's missing. We can't find him anywhere. I don't understand. I was watching the den the entire time! Brezin wasn't far. I… Carlin I… I don't–"

"Stop! Breathe. We don't know anything yet. Let's see if the others can find him."

The pack scoured half our territory, but we never found Vinsi. Worse yet, we found the scents of humans instead. Unlike the ones I'd known before, this trail sent my hackles rising every time I found it. Something was different about these humans. Something my instincts didn't like.

My insides hurt more as soon after, two more of the same litter vanished. Once again, the pack had been out hunting. This time, I'd stayed with Brezin to stand guard. With him outside, I thought it safe to nap when the pups had fallen asleep. I was wrong. I went to sleep with Harso and Marron beside me. I woke up to them gone. Apparently, Tital had made a sprint for the forest, forcing Brezin to chase after him. The other two must have used this break to sneak out themselves.

Their trail went cold near more human trails. Brezin blamed himself. I told him not to. This litter was more spirited than any I'd had before. They'd also been slow to adopt our names for some reason. Truth is, I blamed myself more. Nine years, six of them with pups. I should be doing better. I shouldn't be losing pups like this.

Unfortunately, hunting was hard. We didn't have the numbers for large prey without leaving only one or two to watch the remaining pups. But it had been under such light guard that they'd gotten away. I found myself trapped between horrible choices. I had to feed my pack or no one would survive. But in order to feed my pack, I had to risk the current littler running off again.

As we prepared another hunt, Husita made the choice easy.

"If they are not wise enough to stay, then perhaps they should be allowed to learn."

I very nearly fainted on the spot. "We're losing *pups,* Husita! We're losing our next generation. How can that not matter to you?"

"It *does* matter. But Carlin, think about how much you've scolded, yelled at, and bitten them to stay. Yet here we are, three gone of their own choosing. If they are this foolish now, they won't get smarter later."

"They're our future. I can't abandon them."

"If you don't feed your pack now, there will be no future for *anyone.*"

That's when I knew what I had to do. I was terrified, but after several failed attempts to find small prey, I had no choice. Despite Husita suggesting otherwise, and an inner voice screaming she was right, I left Brezin and Lonate with the remaining pups. I then led the rest of the pack on a hunt. It took us half the day to find a good trail, though it led us to the best possible hunt. A single buck, a bit small perhaps, though more than enough for our pack. Better still, one hind leg was already badly broken. In two moons time, the pups could have taken this one themselves.

As it was, Husita and I charged in on our own. We went in with a leap's distance between us. The same tactic that had allowed us to hunt so successfully when it was only us. Like so many times before, we held ourselves from full sprint. We were waiting for the prey to make its choice.

It chose her. The buck turned and thrust its antlers at her. She dodged away, keeping the buck's attention. Meanwhile, I had accelerated to my full sprint. I went in straight for its neck. By the time it remembered me, it was too late. My jaws found its throat. I clamped down as hard as I could. I intended to drain the life from him as I had so many times before. Instead, I'd found such a good hold I actually snapped his neck right there. He collapsed in a heap, almost falling on top of me. I held my hold long enough to be sure before I panted exertion from the sprint.

"Lucky bite," Husita said.

"I'll take any luck I can get these days," I said.

"I'll take some meat back to the pups."

"No, eat up first."

Husita's ears shifted, though I'm not sure why. "Are you sure? With what's been going on, shouldn't I go back?"

"I'd rather have you well fed first. Besides, as you said, if they can't wisen up, perhaps it's best to leave them to their fate."

Her ears shifted uncomfortably, but she began feeding with the rest of us.

In truth, my insides weren't so sure. Half said I was right. The other half said I needed to go back *now*! Neither side could gain an edge, so I went with the immediate issue. I hadn't had a good meal in a long time. If these pups continued their activities, I would need all the strength I could get to keep up. That and I was confident that either Lonate and Brezin would keep them safe, or they would disappear no matter what I did.

Once we'd eaten our fill, we tore off parts of the kill for the rest of the pack. I admit I did press us to move faster, just in case that other half of me was right. I didn't think it was though. We'd be fine. The pack would be fine.

I couldn't have been more wrong.

We arrived to find the area completely empty. No pups, older or younger. Husita went inside the den, and came out confirming they were all gone. The others checked for trails while I checked every tree and bush with my eyes. I lifted my head in a long howl to call them back. I made it sound as frantic as I could, hoping it might spur the older pair to return no matter what.

Nothing happened. No response, and no sign of them.

"Something happened," I said as much to myself as to the others. "Lonate wouldn't abandon the meeting area. Not without good reason. Something… something…"

"Carlin! Calm down," Husita said, "We don't know anything. Gulino has a trail. Let's see where it leads. Maybe we can— "

Craack!-cshoo-shoo

All ears turned toward the sounds of thunder. I knew what it was. I'd heard it before while watching the previous pack of humans. This was their thunder sticks. My heart wanted to fly toward the sound. My sense wanted to run the other direction just as fast.

Both warred with themselves when Lonate burst out of the brush in a panicked sprint. His ears were flat, his tail merged with his rear, he looked so terrified he might faint. I think he only stopped in front of me because some part of him didn't want to run me over.

Might have been better if he did. Sometimes pain can cut through fear.

"They… they…" he was barely forming words. "Brezin… he… they… the thunder…"

I hoped some hard words might do it instead. "Lonate! Snap out of it. What's going on? What happened? Where is Brezin?"

"He… we found them… but he… thunder… blood… he fell where…"

His ears shot up so fast I thought they might grow longer. He was looking into the brush as if it might eat him alive. Then without a word, he tore the opposite direction as scared as he'd arrived. Panic struck me, though for no reason I could understand. *What in Wolfor's fang is going on?!*

"Lonate! Where are you going? What happened to— "

CRACK!-CHSHOO-sh-CRACRACK!-CHSOO-shoo-shoo.

Yelps echoed with the thunder. I flinched and turned after the first, only to have my shoulder scream agony with the second.

My heart hurt almost as much. Gulion was dead. His eyes stuck open with blood trickling down from between his eyes. Husita was whining equal pain, carrying a hind leg. Mukala, the other pack member, was going to her to help her.

I knew what had happened. I knew what the injuries were. I also knew how very serious our situation was. We had to leave, now! We had to get away before—

CRACK-CHSOO-shoo-shoo.

Mukala fell. Her whines confirmed she wasn't dead, but she couldn't stand. She could barely find her breath. I went toward Husita first. I tried to keep her moving. I saw the humans come out of the brush. I saw a thunder stick level. I pushed Husita. I tried to get her moving. I tried—

CRACK-CHSOO-shoo-shoo.

I don't know what's worse. Knowing you're about to die, or what I got instead.

Just before the thunder, Husita screamed agony. She pushed off on her injured leg to leap between me and the human. Then she fell. A hole in her side. She didn't make a sound. She simply collapsed. At least her eyes were closed. Maybe they'd closed when she leapt. I don't know. I only know that my mate… my eternal faith… was dead at my paws.

Instinct took over. It drew me into the brush after Lonate. I heard one last crack of thunder, and I knew what it meant. Mukala was dead. My pack was dead. My mate… my pups… all of them… gone.

All but one.

It was a short while before I found Lonate. Long enough for me to be sure the humans weren't chasing me any more. Long enough for the adrenaline to fade, and let me feel.

Lonate… he was shaking like a leaf in a storm. His ears and tail still hadn't come up. He seemed less panicked, but no less afraid.

So many things ran through my head. So many questions, so many emotions, so much pain. Most of it went by without me noticing. The rest hurt too much to retain. Only one thing survived the maelstrom.

"What… happened?"

Lonate looked at me as if I were some… I don't know… scary… thing.

"We… we found the others. Altin and Tital… they got away. We decided to let them and follow, hoping they might lead us to the others."

"You let them slip away? Without me there?!"

"It worked though! We found them all. The entire litter. They were trapped by some kind of… spider web?… I don't know what it was. They couldn't chew through it, neither could we. Then… then… those two-legged things. They came out of the forest. Brezin and I, we challenged them. We snarled at them, trying to chase them away. Then… then… then thunder. Thunder like none I've ever heard. It came from a stick one of them had in their paws. Brezin, he… he… he just… died! Fell down right where he stood. Not even a yip. When the stick pointed at me, I ran. I felt something scratch my back. I kept running. Then I… I… I had to come home. I had to find safety. I… I…"

I don't know if he ever said another word. If he did, I never heard it. My pups… no doubt dead now. Killed by the humans. My pack… also dead. Killed by the humans. The first was their own fault. The second… Lonate… he'd led them back. He'd led them to us, then didn't stay to fight. If he had, we might have won, or been able to run. His fault. His fault my pack was dead. His fault Husita was dead. His fault… his…

Don't even think it.

It's already done.

"Get out."

Lonate froze solid at my voice. It had come out as much a snarl as words. I don't know if he didn't understand, or didn't believe. I intended to rectify both.

"Leave my territory. Do not let me find your scent again. You are a lone wolf now. You will never know the company of another wolf. You will live your life forever alone!"

His eyes bulged at me as shock took him. "Carlin. Carlin please no. Please, I'm sorry. I didn't… I… father— "

"Don't father me! My pack is dead because of you! They died because you did not stand and fight. When they died, you ran. You…

you're a coward. You don't deserve to be called a wolf. You deserve a death worse than the pack you abandoned. And by Wolfor's fang, if I ever see you again, I will make sure you face that death!"

He shook so much it's a wonder I didn't feel it. Maybe I did. All I could see was the blood of my pack... of Husita... on his jaws. His fault. His fault! *His fault!* He deserved to die for what he did! When he didn't move, I went for him as if I might make good on my threat. He sprinted away even faster than he'd run before. I didn't chase him. I didn't have the heart. It was dead out there by my den. Husita. My ever lasting faith. Dead, because of one of her own.

Chapter 4

It's your own fault and you know it!

Please leave me alone.

The only trail I could find was a rabbit. It made a decent meal, but did nothing to fill the void within.

What have I done?

It rang over and over in my head. It hadn't stopped since my grief had faded enough for my memory to return. Enough for me to remember what I'd done.

Lonate. My son. What I'd said... what I'd done... *Wolfor forgive me! Help me find him. Help me make it right!* I prayed every day. I don't know if I was ever heard.

It wasn't his fault. If anything, it was mine. My instincts had said Husita needed to remain behind, then they said I needed to return, but I ignored them both times. I knew better. Wolfor's fang, *I knew better*! Now my pack was dead. Lonate did go wrong, but I... I had done much worse. I had banished him. Declared him a lone wolf. For nothing! For being a young pup too afraid to think. For being in a position he never should have been.

I should have stayed, or Husita, or anyone. Someone with experience should have stayed while I took a pup with me on the hunt. Lonate had done that maneuver before. He could have helped me with the kill. But no. I wanted the best hunter. I was sure the pups would be fine.

I was a stupid, idiotic fool!

And now I couldn't rectify my error. I had gone after Lonate. I wanted to find him, to revoke his sentence. To apologize. To... I don't even know. He needed me. He needed someone to help him grieve... so did I. He was all I had left, and I had chased him away.

He never responded to my howls. His trail went cold, so I tried to hold that direction. He'd gone in a straight line since, so maybe I'd find him. My need to hunt threw me off. Even as I tried, I knew I'd strayed. I kept praying though. I begged Wolfor to forgive me. Begged him to watch over Lonate.

Begged him to do the latter at the expense of the former, if that's what it took.

After moons of searching, I had to admit the truth. I'd lost him. Was he alone? Was he dead? I'm not sure I even wanted to know. I kept praying however. I didn't know what else to do. All I could do was... stay alive.

Time turned my pain into scars. I found a way to find joy, though it rarely came without Husita sneaking into the moment. Though in a way, it helped. It was as if I still had a part of her with me. I knew better, though every now and then a breeze would ruffle my fur, and I'd think... I'd imagine, maybe she really was there. It was all I had.

The howls of other wolves soon filled the forest. Other packs had come. At times, I thought I heard Lonate, though his voice was still maturing when last I heard him. Could well be my heart wishing for the impossible. Early on in my search for him, I'd found the remains of one pack that had starved. Seemed odd considering one of them was a solid black wolf so huge I thought he was a bear at first. A wolf like that could take down healthy bulls alone, yet the pack had starved. With their failure in mind, I was curious about these other packs I had found a great distance away. I had no right to join them, but that didn't mean I couldn't watch.

Though I ran into something else first.

I was just waking from a nap inside a rock pile that was more the remains of a landslide. Didn't matter really. It was a comfortable place to sleep, and that's all I'd wanted.

As I woke, I saw a young wolf right outside my "den" hunting a fox. Well, trying to. I knew he was going to mess it up long before he did. He was tracking it like he would anything else. Poor wolf.

I knew from experience you couldn't sneak up to a fox. You had to out-chase it. You had to reach full speed before it knew you were there.

The wolf himself was interesting though. His pelt was mostly silver, with his hackles being almost pure silver to the point of becoming a sort of… I don't know… silver sheen, for lack of better description. It was outlined in a very tiny smattering of black on his back, which only served to highlight it more.

In a way he reminded me of Vinsi. Something about him made me think he had a similar spirit. Seemed like he was a capable hunter, he'd just never hunted a fox before. I watched a little while longer, wondering if maybe he'd wise up in time. No sooner did I think it than he proved me right the first time. He took one step too many. The fox heard him, saw him, and dashed away into the morning fog.

The young wolf sighed his frustration, and I saw his whole life in his eyes. It was as if I were looking into myself. I could see all the pain and loneliness I'd felt since I lost my pack a second time. I could see his ears searching for the paws of his pack to catch the kill he'd missed, even though he knew they weren't there. It was all so ingrained in his fur, only a fool would think him alone for a short time. It radiated from him in one motion as his body sank with the sigh. I suddenly felt like I'd known him since he was a pup. I also knew, all at once, what I was going to do. First, if he reacted the right way, I'd have some fun with him. Then I'd get to know him enough to find out why he'd been alone for so long.

And I knew, with out a doubt, that this was a beginning for both of us.

So I rose, drew myself up even though he couldn't see me, and I spoke loud and clear so that my voice echoed among the rocks.

"Next time, try attacking before it hears you. That is the only way to catch a fox."

At first he was startled out of his fur. Didn't run though, which was promising. In fact, his ears quickly softened from fearful attention to curious.

"Who's in there?" he said. "Who, or rather what, are you?"

I think we can have our fun with him.

I agree. He won't like it though.

He'll live.

"I am old, I am wise. I am the Wise One," I said. "I am like you, young wolf: a loner."

The young wolf ruffed disgust at me. "Right. A rock pile is like me. I ask again: who's in there? Show yourself."

I walked out slowly, trying to... I guess appear timeless or something. Maybe it was silly, but it felt right, so I went with it.

"Call me, 'the Wise One,'"

"Wise One?" the young wolf said. "Yeah right. You're just an old wolf finding fun in tormenting us younger ones. You don't know anything about me."

If only he knew.

He'll learn.

"Are you sure? I have lived for eleven years. I know much more than you do. Like how to catch a fox and suffer very little."

Now his ears flicked dismissal. *Maybe I tried to have too much fun.* "Oh, well, good for you. I'm only three years old, and I've felt the pain of losing everything I have. My home, my family, my heart. I know what it feels like to be shunned by every one I once knew. You don't know anything about that."

My ears flashed back as I remembered my own banishment. I wasn't certain that's what he meant but somehow, I got the feeling, it was. Regardless, the pain of those years, and of the years most recent, came back in a rush. I felt and remembered it all and this time, I felt like I really was a "Wise One".

"Actually, I do," I said, sounding somewhat regal without intending to.

He responded with a fierce snarl. "You can't. I was falsely accused of killing my brother. For that, I was kicked out of my pack. Every wolf in these woods knows of me, and they shun me more than my own. I am cursed to live alone, forever. What do you have to say about that?"

More than you'll ever know!

I stared him down. Not angry, not reprimanding, not even painful. My gaze bore into him as if I might transfer my soul into his. My pups had called it my teaching glare, though I'd also used it to simply gain attention.

Worked on him in a different way. His snarl faded. His ears softened from aggression to attention. While tension remained in him, it wasn't as strong as before.

"I was banished as well," I said. "My life was a lonely one until a female showed her support for me. We mated and started our own pack. I was happy even though I thought it impossible. I made a difference in her life. No one else would have her but me."

"Get to the point, Old One."

Trying to break my control? Good luck pup. I continued as if he hadn't said a word. "Lone wolf or not, you can make a difference. It may be small, or it may be big, but you *can* make a difference. Just as I did."

He may not have broken my control, but apparently, *I* had broken *his* patience.

"Whatever 'Wise One'," he said. "You old wolves are stubborn, so I won't argue. I'll leave you to you and your small difference."

I growled at him, now very much angry with his tone, and his insult. It wasn't just me he'd insulted. He had insulted himself too. He didn't understand what I was trying to tell him. I didn't like it, nor was I about to give up on him.

"I'm not done with you yet."

"Yes you are!"

He ran off before I could say anything further.

I think we tried too hard.

I think you're right.

So are we giving up?

Nope. But maybe we won't be so "wise" from now on.

More than ever, I was certain his fate was similar to mine. Was he really innocent? Both sides of me agreed, that too was definite. While his punishment had left him bitter, he didn't seem the kind of wolf to kill anyone without reason. More to the point, here was a young wolf who was hurting. That sigh, it wasn't just about the failed hunt. It was everything he'd endured since being banished.

I could just imagine Lonate doing the same. I couldn't help him now, but maybe by helping this young wolf I could make amends. It was shallow, it was weak, and it was all I had.

Thus, I went searching for him. Took some time, and a lot of tracking, before his trail led me to him. Or rather his den, which stood as proof that Wolfor has a sense of humor. This young wolf had claimed a small rock pile as his "den". Not the worst choice I suppose for a lone wolf. Stone didn't erode, and you could sharpen your claws on its walls.

He must have run into some kind of trouble since I last saw him too. The trail I'd found had several drops of blood in it, and every drop was still wet. Yet there were no constant streams or large drops, which told me the wounds were likely minor. Though I couldn't help remembering how hard minor wounds felt before Husita found me, so I decided to reserve judgment as far as how he was taking it.

That said, I couldn't help having just a little more fun with him. I stood outside his den, drew myself up all big and proud, raised tail included, even though I knew he couldn't see me. Then, I tried once again to sound timeless, or whatever it was I sounded like before.

Sadly this time, it just came out as old, "I told you I wasn't done with you."

Epilogue

I was just settling in for a nap after our round of mouse hunting when Estrella, Luna's mate, came running toward me. My ears perked as she approached. *Now what?*

"Carlin," she said. "Luna needs us. Rajor's pack is in the field past Luna's markings. I don't think he'll leave quietly."

I didn't bother with questions. The young wolf I'd met not so long ago needed me. The only detail I cared about was the danger involved the brother that had gotten him banished. If nothing else, I had to get my first look at this Rajor I'd heard so much about.

That alone would have had me jumping to my paws.

"Lead the way!" I said.

Estrella turned, and I followed without a word. On the way, I realized just how much Luna likely needed me. I had no doubt we were headed for a territorial dispute. Luna and Estrella were young, but I'd yet to see them fight, and we were almost certainly outnumbered. They would need my experience if a fight broke out. True it had been a while since I fought another wolf, but I wasn't so old that I couldn't handle myself. Well, not yet anyway.

When we arrived, I saw a black wolf standing among the field of dead leaves we'd been hunting in just a moment before. From Luna's description, this was no doubt his brother Rajor. On his own, not much trouble, except a small hunting party was a short distance away. A half dozen or so adults, with the current litter gathered tight near by. They and their guardians were watching their alpha as he and Luna stared at each other.

Okay, this could be trouble if a real fight breaks out.

Changes nothing.

No, just pointing out the odds.

Luna and Estrella exchanged a rub while I kept my head low to get a better look at Rajor. I looked him over hair by hair, and by Wolfor's tail, I could not understand. There was no aura there, no confidence. His eyes looked too many ways, his fur didn't stand straight enough, and after my many years of fighting wolves, I was able to evaluate his fighting ability long before Estrella and Luna had stopped rubbing. I suppose this Rajor had his points, but alpha? Him?! Brezin could have taken him the day he died. Fully grown... Wolfor's fang, he'd have pinned Rajor in his sleep.

"Is this the brother you've told me so much about?" I said.

Luna looked at Rajor a moment before replying. "Yes. This is Rajor."

"How did a whelp like that ever make alpha?"

Rajor growled at me while his fur started to rise.

"Careful what you say, Old Fool. My patience has limits."

I looked at Luna before turning my ears back almost laughing. Luna had said almost the exact same thing only a short time ago. Maybe they were brothers after all.

"As does mine," Luna said. "You will not hunt here. Take your pack and leave. Do not violate my territory again."

Rajor's tail finally began to rise, though it was still far short of a proper display. "Speaking of violations, do your companions know about your sentence? What you did?"

Is he really trying that?

I think he's really trying that.

Estrella didn't skip a beat. "Yes, we do."

I wasn't far behind. "And we don't care about lies."

To his credit, Rajor wasn't backing down, and his hackles were starting to rise as well. Yet there was still just enough doubt, or fear, to keep them from reaching their full display.

"The only lies are the ones he's apparently told you. He killed his own brother as a pup. For his crime, he was made a lone wolf. He is destined to live alone, to never know the company of another wolf. You risk—"

Wolfor's fang, give it up already.

"Shut up, pup. We're not listening. Now, I suggest you heed Luna's command before you feel our fangs."

Rajor managed a glare, and a stiffness, that was actually fairly impressive. I could imagine it working on a lot of wolves I'd met over the years. The only problem was he was glaring at me, Luna, and Estrella. Any one of us were his better twice over, and we knew it. The more he glared, the more I began to wonder if deep down, he knew it too.

"Do not underestimate me," Rajor said. "My position is mine by virtue of my strength. I go where I wish. I hunt, where I wish. No murderer will dictate what I can or cannot do."

Luna ruffed amusement with a sideways glance at Estrella. "This... murderer... has chosen what mate you *won't* have. Why couldn't he also say the same about your territory?"

Nice one, Luna.

Rajor sprinted straight for Luna, blood on his jaws. Luna rushed to meet him with a snarl of his own to match. I tensed to join the fight, except the other pack wasn't moving. Indeed, their only response was their pup-sitter yelling at his alpha.

"Rajor stop! You have pups here! You can't risk a fight! *Rajor!*"

Had a fight broken out, I would have joined it. I would have put my life on the line to protect Luna, who I only then realized I saw as my alpha. Had Rajor gained the advantage, I would have watched the fight to ensure my alpha survived.

None of that ever happened. I never for a second doubted Luna's ability, or that the other pack would remain where they stood. Thus, when I recognized the voice that had cried out between us, my eyes and ears latched onto him.

Lonate? No. No, it couldn't be. Not after what I did to him.

A part of my mind kept an eye on the fight, but Luna had full control, making it barely an afterthought.

Even as my heart and mind refused to accept it, my eyes couldn't deny it. There he was. Lonate. My son. The pup *I* had wronged. The pup that I... what will he say? How will he react?

I never found out, because he never did. The pups were too stirred by the fight. Despite getting help, Lonate had to work hard to keep them contained. I don't know if he never saw me, or was too busy to react. Perhaps it's just as well. He'd have every right to turn the pack on me. Or to ignore me as a final justice.

As for me, everything I wanted to do I couldn't. I wanted to go to him. I wanted to feel his fur against mine, to take in his scent. I wanted to apologize. I wanted to beg for his forgiveness. I wanted him to... to know I never meant what I'd said.

As Luna won the fight, I kept my stare on Lonate. It hurt as much as the day I lost him. As the pack began gathering to leave, I knew I would never see him again, but it wouldn't be because of him.

I knew my body. I knew I didn't have many years left. Luna had teased me about it, but it was true. I was an old wolf. I'd be seeing Wolfor fairly soon. Still, Lonate... How much I wanted to rush to him, to feel him one last time. Yet I knew I couldn't. My desire kept me watching. Truth kept me in place.

He had a new pack now. One that obviously trusted him. He wouldn't demand that much control over the pups if he didn't. I always knew he had a talent for pup-sitting. I just didn't realize how much. He had a good life now. If I were to go to him...

You'd ruin it.

I know. Doesn't make it easier.

We don't deserve easy.

We were right. I felt it the moment I thought it. Wolfor had answered my prayers... in full. Lonate had been given a new life. A proper, happy life. Me? I suddenly had a feeling my end wouldn't be so easy. *So be it.* I deserved a lot for my errors. For tainting the blood of an alpha by my actions.

I kept watching long after Lonate was gone. Knowing I'd never see him again hurt as if my legs had been chewed off. Knowing he'd found such a high place in a pack made it worth it.

Farewell, Lonate. I'm sorry. I hope someday, you can forgive me.

Later, in my final moments, I would feel Wolfor's muzzle. As I breathed my last, I would know that by helping Luna, I had redeemed myself. That he would go on to do good things. With my final breath, I knew that words of advice I'd had for him, were meant for me as well.

"Even a lone wolf can do good things."

About the Author

Forest Wells is an author with dysgraphia, but those things don't go together, which is why he did it anyway. He specializes in stories that focus on the emotions and personal journeys characters face regardless of the genre he's writing. All of which is fueled by his deep passions for all things wild canine, sci-fi and fantasy, and really any well told story. When he's not writing, or helping with his parent's Girl Scout troops, you'll find him watching his favorite NFL and NHL teams, watching E-sports, or gaming himself. Assuming he's not caught up in the biggest of all procrastinating tools: Twitter. His first novel "Luna, The lone Wolf" was released in April of 2019, but he had a few short stories and poems published in anthologies before that. He currently lives in his home town of Thermal, California.

You've read the origins, but did you read the original tale?

Luna, The Lone Wolf

Luna was destined to be alpha once he became an adult, but before he got the chance, his own brother, Rajor, framed him for a crime no one committed, leading to Luna being banished from the pack. Declared a lone wolf, never to know the company of another wolf, Luna turns bitter as he learns to accept his new fate. Yet even as he does, other wolves, strange two-legged creatures, and one mockingbird, force themselves into his life, driving him through a gauntlet of trials where he must reconnect with the alpha he was born to be, or turn away from it forever – assuming he survives.

Available now in paper back and E-book.

www.ingramcontent.com/pod-product-compliance
Ingram Content Group UK Ltd.
Pitfield, Milton Keynes, MK11 3LW, UK
UKHW042018190726
13854UKWH00005B/2355

9 781733 712439